Vixen

The Gamer's Girlfriend

Ida Brady

This is a work of fiction. The events described are fictitious; any
similarities to actual events and persons are coincidental.

Editing by Hilary Manning
Proofreading by Norma Gambini
Cover design by DAZED Designs
Formatting by Ebony McKenna

www.idabrady.com

Chapter One

Emmaline purred in her sleep.

She was having the most delicious dream. One that made the ache between her thighs feel so very real.

He was there. She could feel the heat of him, smell the sandalwood and sweat on his body. It aroused her beyond measure.

"Do not toy with me, Your Grace."

"Ah, but don't you see, my sweet?" His hand traveled down her chin, descending until it stopped just shy of one breast, heaving beneath her nightgown. "There is a delicious thrill in teasing. It tunes the body, like that of a violinist with his strings. Tweaking, adjusting, until the perfect note can be played. You will soon learn that it makes the doing all the more sweet."

She moaned then pressed her hand against her mound, shifting her hips. She craved his fullness, yearned for the meeting of flesh to flesh.

"Oh," she sighed as the jolt passed through her.

Emmaline arched off the bed, rubbing at the small, sensitive flesh through her nightgown. With every stroke, the fabric grew damp. The sensation of William's mouth on her neck, his wicked words against her throat, urging her on, would make the devil proud.

He nibbled at her ear, biting and sucking until she cried out. It felt so wonderfully real. Like he was solid flesh.

Emmaline's eyes flew open.

This was no dream.

She must have fallen asleep waiting for his arrival. She had seen him at her uncle's private dinner and every moment in his presence left her in agony. Ever since their wicked carriage ride, Emmaline had craved more. She had managed to speak to His Grace just as the ladies retired—long enough to invite him to a more private interlude.

"I thought you would not come."

His answer was a wicked grin, a flash of heat and desire before he pounced.

She moaned when his tongue stroked hers in a kiss that was as scandalous as their passion.

He was in her bedchamber. He was in her bed.

"Nothing could keep me away," William muttered, wrenching his mouth from hers. "I keep my word, Emmaline. And I understood your invitation clearly."

Emmaline bit her lip. "Nothing is beyond your comprehension."

"Not when it comes to matters of the flesh. And

given the nature of your activities while you slept, I am glad I was not further delayed."

Emmaline could naught but gasp before he kissed her once more.

To be held in his arms, to feel the strong, capable bands of muscle enfolding her, holding her tight, only heightened her desire. She longed for this intimacy, the way his hard muscle pressed against her, the complete assurance that he could take take take.

And she would give.

She no longer cared that they may be discovered; she no longer feared being found coupling in her bed-chamber. Emmaline embraced this excitement, the wonder of his mouth and hands on her body. She would seek it out with every opportunity.

Maddern speared his hands through her hair, up-setting the neat braid set by her maid. She was deliri-ous, the quivering need insistent now.

"You have the most delectable pair of . . ." William grinned, teasing her nipples. "They are perfect. And just the right size to do this."

He grazed her breasts through the soft cotton of her nightgown. His tongue swirled patterns on the straining peaks until she was tugging his hair, chanting barely decipherable words in the darkness of the room.

When William leaned back, she had to grip the sheets beneath her to keep her hands in place.

"What mysterious thoughts course through your mind?"

"What? No 'tell me your thoughts, wench?'"

Maddern's laughter rang through the quiet, warming her.

The low candle placed beside her bed illuminated his features. Her heart turned at the sight of his humor, at the playful expression across his face. Oh, how she longed for him. Longed to be his in every sense of the word.

The darkness of the room, the forbidden nature of their lovemaking, added another layer to their intimacy. What would it be like to wake beside him? To share the marriage bed knowing that every night, her husband would attend to her?

Bitter, bitter dreams taunted her so.

Slowly, ever so carefully, William ran his hands up under her nightgown. Her heart jackhammered in her chest. She craved fast. Desired frenzy. Instead, he took his time, brushing the inside of her thigh with the back of his fingers, sending her need spiraling ever higher. When he looked up at her with a hungry intensity, the fire that burned inside her became an inferno. That one covetous look melted any reservation that might have lingered.

"Your scent entices me. Like the most aromatic of dishes. The sweetest honey."

He climbed up her leg, drawing her gown with it.

Emmaline held her breath, unable to stop her heart from racing. The expectation of his mouth on her there, in the most intimate of places, was almost too much to bear.

Maddern hovered. His breath warmed her naked thigh.

She was lost in him. In the heady rush that coursed through her body when he was near.

"Please."

William drew back slightly, watching her. A wolfish grin appeared. "Begging already? Tell me, my sweet, what would you have me do to you?"

She was emboldened by his request, excited by the lick of desire that pulsed through her.

"I-I want to brush my body against yours. To feel your hard length pressed against me . . . I want to—"

"Yes?"

"To taste you."

Emmaline kept her head held high. Sharing those intimate thoughts with her lover was the most natural feeling in the world.

William muttered. "What else?"

Emmaline faltered. "I—are you . . ."

"Damnation, woman!" *Maddern gripped her hips, crushing his erection against her.* "Do you feel this? Can you know of my agony?"

"Oh . . ."

"What else would you have me do to you?"

"I want to watch you taste me. To see your tongue do . . . that . . ." *Her chest heaved. She wanted more than anything to feel his naked flesh against her.*

"What?" *Maddern ground out, his jaw set.*

"You know what." *She could not speak the words. Merciful heavens, she was at her limit.*

"Here?" He pressed his hand against her mound. Emmaline gasped, body tense, suspended in need. "Lower."

"Here?"

The pressure. His firm, hard fingers found the spot.

"Yes," she sobbed, relief rushing through her at an alarming rate. She thought she might faint from the force of it. Could one die from too much pleasure? It seemed a cruel fate.

"I want to feel—oh!" The climbing began, a thrilling race. When it slowed, she opened her mouth to find the words but cried out instead. "I—please, William."

She gripped his dark head, guiding him, urging him to continue. "I want you to lick me until I . . . I want to be naked with you. To feel your thickness. To have you taste my—my—oh!"

She tumbled, lost in the dark, dangerous depths of her desire. Time and place held no meaning. She was enslaved to him, caught in the giddy, wondrous chains he had secured around her body. Around her heart.

Emmaline closed her eyes, shuddering as his fingers mercilessly extended her pleasure.

But still she yearned for more.

She nudged him back and kneeled, unbuttoning his breeches, wasting no time in admiring the length of his erection before she took him in her mouth, enjoying the sounds of his pleasure.

William gripped her shoulders. "Fuck." His voice rumbled through her.

Oh, how it made her yearn for him. To take him inside her, to join together as one.

She maintained the same speed, venturing to cup him now, marveling at the heavy round sacs. His hiss of satisfaction encouraged her to continue.

It was as if he were carved in stone. His jaw was clenched, his body rigid with need, and when those wicked green eyes looked down at her, she was struck by his beauty.

Emmaline's heart twisted in her chest. Words she had no right to say, feelings she had no right to claim swirled through her. Heart heavy, she loved him with her mouth, teasing him with her hands, until he swore, jerking her up and away from him.

"I want to bury myself inside you."

And dragging her over to the wooden trunk at the foot of the bed, he did.

She shivered, kneeling on all fours, her legs spread, her arms resting on the mattress. She was exposed, the nightgown bunched at her hips, while her lover positioned himself behind her.

William spat on his fingers then swirled them around her entrance. Emmaline's legs shook, for now she knew what to expect. And she was giddy with anticipation.

Her nipples ached for his mouth; her body yearned for his cock.

"Hurry. Please."

"Patience, my hellcat."

Spread before him, Emmaline felt wonderfully

wicked. A cat in heat. She all but mewed when she felt the tip of his cock tease her entrance.

And when he slowly thrust inside her, when he plundered her in that slow, steady way, she cried out, muffling her scream against her arm.

Yes. Oh, sweet Lord. Yes.

William grunted. And then that slow, steady pace gave way to something raw.

She could scarce draw breath, she was so full of him. And with every thrust, he impaled himself deep inside. She clenched around him, unable to do naught but hold on as he pummeled her from behind, drawing in and out with wicked speed.

All the while, he whispered words that shocked and thrilled her. Words that sent a trickling wetness down her leg, drenching his thick erection.

"William. I—what is this feeling?"

"Do not fight it."

It was a pressure like she had never known before. An exquisite heaviness. A building. But towards what, she knew not. It was different than the first time, stronger and persistent. The dizzying jolt of desire was unrelenting; he struck a chord deep inside.

And so Emmaline succumbed. And the rolling, tumbling joy of it spread through her. She shuddered and shook, sobbing his name as she let go, helpless against the onslaught. Deliciously caught and held captive.

Emmaline lost control, his name on her lips. And the wetness that trickled down her legs shocked her.

"What is . . ."

"A woman's pleasure."

"Oh."

Never had she felt so beautiful. So wanted.

When William cried out, finding his own pleasure, his own release, she shuddered along with him. It was a wondrous thing to hear his passion, to feel the heavy ropes of his desire against her bare skin.

And when he drew her back against him, his arms securing her to his chest, holding her close, Emmaline shed a solitary tear.

Chapter Two

S avannah returned to reality with a hard thump.

Emerging from the sedative was . . . odd. She held the memories of sex with the Duke as if it had happened. As if she were Emmaline, heart full, body yearning, indulging in a naughty shag in her bedchamber.

And what a shag it had been. Doggy-style on the Regency bed . . .

Savannah walked out of Fantasy Core, blinking into the sunlight in a daze. It took a moment, and then another, for her to orient herself. Fantasy Core. Melbourne. Arcas beside her navigating his wheelchair through the parking lot.

"Everything looks out of place," she commented, shielding her eyes. She glanced around at the cars, the bright-green Fiesta, the rich red Corolla, even the boring grey sedan—all seemed so garish and odd.

"It's because we've been having hot sex as Emmaline and the Duke in Regency England. Everything is going to be a little off."

"But even the sounds, Cas."

"Weird, right?"

"Everything was so *soft*."

"Motors. We're so used to hearing them that we don't even think twice about it."

Savannah shook her head, glancing back at the glass building that glinted in the sunlight. Too modern for her post-Regency sensibilities.

Fantasy Core had been a wonderful cross between science lab and hotel, with staff warm and welcoming but still clinical, down to business. And that business was pleasure— a cutting-edge tech company that specialized in bringing one's fantasy to life.

Any fantasy.

The company used technology that tapped into the nervous system and the brain, resurfacing old memories and imposing them on new ones. Memories and feelings and sensations that triggered responses in the brain that would make her feel like Emmaline, to have Arcas feel like he was screwing her as the Duke —in short, a nervous-system mirage.

When they had been offered a chance to try it out —as part of a social media promotion—Savannah had jumped at the opportunity. Another kinky experience to test? Yes, please.

Savannah brushed her hand along her thigh as she walked towards their car, still expecting to feel the electrodes against her skin. Even with all the positive reviews, a part of her had remained skeptical they would feel anything. But it had worked. She had actually experienced sex with the Duke of Maddern. She had shagged her ultimate book boyfriend. And it had been fucking glorious.

"You felt all that, right? The bedchamber, the sex?" Savannah unlocked the car.

"Every fucking thrust."

Savannah shivered at the heat in Arcas' eyes. She turned to him before starting the engine. "I know we've just had hot Regency sex, but I'm so fucking turned on remembering it."

Arcas flipped his thumb upright. "So am I."

Savannah laughed.

"I hate to break it to you, Van, but I think we're going to be frequent visitors to Fantasy Core," Arcas replied, feigning regret.

"Not with that eye-watering cost."

His green eyes glinted wickedly. "Anything for your pleasure, Van."

"And yours."

Savannah winced when she turned the key in the ignition and the radio blared out some pop song. Everything sounded so harsh to her ears. Even the low hum of the engine was jarring. Fantasy Core had done a fucking fantastic job of making her feel every element of her experience. The soft muslin cotton, the heavy press of the Duke against her bare skin, the rasp of his cheek against hers . . . It was no wonder she was slightly dazed.

"Hey, don't get me wrong, banging you on that four-poster was sexy as fuck, but I'm pretty pumped to try out my fantasy. And kind of relieved that you're open to it." Arcas squeezed her thigh as she pulled out of the lot just ahead of the grey sedan.

They had just lived out Savannah's fantasy—every ducal angle of it. Arcas? His fantasy, he had confided to her on their drive over, was to have dragon sex.

"So how would it work exactly, Cas?"

"Well, you would be the dragon and I would be a handsome warrior man."

Savannah wriggled in the driver's seat, weaving through the back streets, deliberately choosing a less direct route to avoid the Saturday afternoon traffic in the city. "So I get to be a scaly, fire-breathing badass motherfucker?"

Arcas laughed. "You're already pretty fucking badass, Van."

Savannah slipped on her sunglasses. "I'll take that. And before you pump me with questions, of course I'm happy to try out this dragon fantasy."

If this was how she felt coming out of a Regency experience, what would it be like returning to reality after being in the body of a dragon? Savannah wanted to experience everything, and part of her wondered if this was going to be the beginning of an addiction.

Who the hell was she kidding? She was already hooked on this stuff. Fantasy Core just upped the ante.

Savannah bit her lip as she ran through the red light. "Oops."

"Daydreaming instead of driving?"

"Guilty. Shit. But hey, that other car drove through the red light too." Savannah shook her head, trying to focus on the road, but her mind was still giddy with memories of sex with the Duke.

Now that Emmaline and her titled lover had finally gone all the way, there was a shift in Emmaline's desire. While the woman had guts and courage, there was a new confidence there. She felt it as she made love with the Duke. The way she stroked his body, the confidence in teasing him with her mouth . . .

She sensed a wonderful boldness to her, a desire to explore this new world of sex with William. Nothing was out of bounds, nothing too risky.

Because despite the restrictions, Emmaline was risking it all for her chance at happiness. With every interlude, she was putting her reputation on the line, her family name, her supposed 'worth' as a nineteenth-century woman, and she was rejecting every restriction with each new interaction.

Emmaline had grown as a woman, developing an understanding of her desires and her limits. And knowing that the Duke was eager for her, that he would always come back to her, was a giddy thrill.

Savannah bit her lip, remembering the way Maddern had looked at her, touched her . . .

William was no longer the boy who had been influenced by his father—or society—to reject Emmaline when they had been younger. He had grown into a man, a virile, vibrant one who was atoning for the errors of the past. Intent on staking his claim.

The way he had held her close had—

Savannah hit the brakes hard as the car in front of her came to an abrupt stop.

"Shit!"

Arcas' hand shot out, bracing her torso against the seat.

They both jerked as the car halted, stopping just in time. In a panic, Savannah checked her rearview mirror, bracing herself, then breathed a sigh of relief as the sedan behind them stopped just before impact.

The grey sedan.

Savannah frowned.

"Cas." Her voice shook a little.

"What's wrong?" Arcas squeezed her shoulder.

"I think we're being followed."

"What?"

"Don't look!" she said when he whipped his head back.

When the car ahead of them moved off, Savannah nervously accelerated, hands shaking slightly. She turned down a laneway then circled back around again. "That car that stopped behind me was at Fantasy Core. I'm sure of it."

"Breathe. I'm right here."

Savannah's mind raced. Why was someone from Fantasy Core following them? It didn't make sense.

She needed time to think, but her thoughts were as jammed as the afternoon traffic.

"Do you want to pull over?"

"No." She swallowed, the giddy, elated feeling she had been basking in gone. Her stomach twisted, and she rubbed at her chest. Surely she was imagining it?

Savannah shook her head. No. She was certain.

Checking her rearview mirror, Savannah continued to drive slowly, deliberately taking odd turns as they drove back toward the city, with Arcas looking behind them.

"I think he must have turned off a side street."

Savannah nodded, breathing out a little.

But as she stopped in front of their apartment parking lot, waiting for the automatic gate to open, she glanced back one more time. And froze.

The grey sedan shot past them and careened around the corner.

"Fuck!" Arcas glanced at her. "What the hell?"

Savannah pressed her lips together, terror coating the back of her throat.

"I don't know."

And as soon as she said it, the fog cleared. She understood. And the fear she felt was replaced by a sick heartache. Why the hell were they following her? What did they have to gain from this? She thought the silence meant they had moved on. That they would stop telling her how to live her life.

And through the queasy fear was anger, a fiery-hot rage that they thought they could keep tabs on what she was doing. They had no right.

With jaw clenched, Savannah drove through to their parking bay. She only knew of one person who could be responsible for this . . .

Her brother.

Chapter Three

Emmaline could not hide her satisfied smile.

She cared not if the Duke's attentions to her at the opera had caused a ripple amongst the ton. Emmaline had never favored their opinion, and as a spinster, she was certain they had never favored hers.

Until now.

William had dared to speak to her, which in turn had led many other eligible bachelors to similarly act attentive, and suddenly Emmaline was overcome with eager gentlemen wanting to converse with her.

Not that she was interested. There was only one man whose attentions she craved.

She watched him now, caught in conversation with Lady Musgrove. Every so often, his eyes would meet hers, and once more her skin would burn anew.

Emmaline flicked out her fan, cooling her overheated cheeks.

She was at her aunt's ball, she reminded herself,

surrounded by the watchful eyes of the ton—*and yet all she wished was for William to touch her, to take her somewhere secluded and make her wicked dreams come true.*

Her legs trembled as a pair of bold green eyes pinned her. She watched, bosom heaving, as his gaze grazed her lips, kissing the swell of her breasts before burning through her clothes right at the apex of her thighs.

Emmaline controlled her breathing. It was unbearably hot. Perhaps she required some refreshment before her next dance.

She snapped her fan shut and turned toward the refreshment room as a tell-tale blonde approached William and Lady Musgrove. Emmaline bit back a sound of disgust.

"You will have to school your features far better than that, my dear Miss Collins."

Emmaline started as the Earl of Walcott appeared beside her, offering her a knowing smile.

With a disgruntled flick of her wrist, she showcased her fan once more.

"I know not what you mean, my lord."

"That is far better." He gestured to her fan. "A lady must use all her accoutrements to guard her feelings during the Season."

"Why is that, my lord?"

Walcott gestured to the ladies and gentlemen gathered at her aunt's ball. "All those matchmaking mammas and eager young chits ready to draw blood."

"Indeed."

Walcott shuddered. "It is a ghastly business, this matter of marriage. I can only be thankful that the Season is drawing to a close."

"As am I."

Walcott smiled rakishly. "And here I thought this Season's delights had been highly . . ." Walcott gestured. ". . . educational."

Emmaline had the grace to blush. Memories of Walcott rutting a woman at the Cyprian ball flashed through her mind. Educational indeed.

"I have had a very successful Season. Perhaps not by the ton's standards, but nonetheless highly enjoyable."

"And you have had a most excellent tutor. Though I suppose I am not as lucky as Maddern this Season."

"Oh?" Emmaline watched as Lady Dewberry greeted William. Her own fingers curled. Her dress, made of the finest muslin, felt scratchy and hot at her breasts. She wished to tear it off her chest and run naked and free across the crowded room.

She glanced at Walcott instead and stiffened at his enigmatic expression as he answered: "I should think it obvious, no?"

Before them, Lady Dewberry reached forward to place her hand on Maddern's forearm, whispering something of a private nature. Emmaline watched, alarmed. There was an air of familiarity about her. Of intimacy. Of the same seemingly heated understanding that William had directed her way.

Vixen

How could that be?

"Every duke must eventually find his duchess," Walcott continued, also watching.

Emmaline's smile faltered. "Duchess?"

The Duke and Lady Dewberry.

William and that woman.

Was Walcott somehow warning her of Maddern's plans?

Her stomach heaved. She itched to tear at Lady Dewberry's fashionably high-waisted gown. To rail and cry out in protest.

He is mine. He is mine. He is mine.

The warm and wonderful feelings she had held close to her chest oozed out, as if she had been pierced by a dagger, wounded and weak. Whatever had happened to the happy, satisfied Emmaline? The one confidently moving on with her life?

She stole an unsteady breath. Had what she feared come to fruition? Oh, it was intolerable to think on it, but think she must. And not in this overcrowded room.

"Pray, excuse me." Emmaline curtseyed, excusing herself.

Was it really such a shock? William required a wife, one with a title and fortune whom he could marry and parade about society as the mother of his children. What he could not do was claim his mistress as a duchess.

And what was she, but his mistress? The woman whose virginity he had taken in a carriage after exposing her to the behavior of his debauched friend?

Emmaline gasped as she careened into a solid male chest.

William. He was standing before her now, no longer conversing with Lady Dewberry.

Devil take him!

His scent surrounded her, earthy and enticing. His hands—though brief—stole out to steady her. She was branded by that contact. Eager to have it again.

But she was also very much aware of their position in public. And of the sly assessment of Lady Dewberry even as she followed the Duke across the room, her eyes ever-fixed on him.

"Miss Collins, I believe I have the honor of this next dance."

"I—" Emmaline looked up, desperately trying to remain calm. "Yes. I had not forgotten."

Before her, Maddern frowned. Nonetheless, he bowed and led her back into the ballroom. Along with her heart.

"It is a country dance, I believe. Nothing so scandalous as a waltz," William murmured close.

Emmaline's lips curved, humor and shock wrestling for purchase.

She longed only to take the aching pain in her chest and cast it out to sea. To let it sink to the bottom of the ocean and with it, any hope to which she had clung.

"Penny for your thoughts?" William asked as he took his position in the set.

Immediately, Emmaline was flooded with images

of them in the carriage. Before they had . . . Those had been the very same words he had spoken to her then.

She snuck a glance at his face, at the satisfied expression, and knew he had spoken those words to rouse her. Oh! He had the very devil in him—in such a public place—to dare reference their lovemaking.

Perhaps she was turning wicked.

Emmaline stepped towards him, then back, counting her steps, willing her mind to remain rational. Reasoned.

But all that flashed before her were images of the Duke, his face in raptures, as she writhed above him in the carriage. His hands on her hips, his mouth on her breasts. He had uttered those words to her, drawing out her confession. Her need for him.

She was a fallen woman. She would always now be a fallen woman. But no matter the outcome of this Season, she would never regret being William's lover. How could she when it brought her so much joy?

"I was thinking on the success of the Season."

Maddern's eyebrows shot up. A sardonic smile curled at his lip.

"Is that so?"

"Indeed. Lord Walcott and I were speaking on it. And I am in agreement. It will be a relief once the Season is over and we are able to return to our regular schedules."

"And do you—" William grimaced as they parted, skirting around the couple beside them to face one another once more. "And what does a 'regular schedule' entail for you?"

Emmaline lifted her chin. "I shall return to my family's home in Wiltshire, perhaps take up a situation as a governess. I have not thought that far ahead." She lifted her own eyebrow now.

"Surely your sister's wedding will keep you in town?"

"Only long enough for the wedding breakfast and to wish them well on their bridal tour. My father is not keen on London. The distance is far too great for his constitution."

William's jaw clenched, his expression shifting from teasing to terse.

Oh, how cruel for her heart to leap at such a scowl. Where she should be trembling with fear, there was excitement. Where she should feel distressed, there was desire.

This was what it was to be in love with the Duke.

Dizzying, delightful, and utterly confounding.

"And when will the banns be read?"

"Their last reading will be Sunday week."

They danced in silence then, to the point that Emmaline almost gave up conversation. But her body . . . her body betrayed her, communicating with him with every rhythmic beat. The warmth of his hand kissing hers, the brush of his shoulder teasing hers, every part of her body gravitated towards his, eager for more contact.

"And what do you want?"

"Why do you wish to know? I would think it is of no consequence to you."

The Duke's eyes flickered. "I respectfully disagree. Do you enjoy London? Or do you prefer the country?"

"I find the recent attention from various gentlemen diverting, but I do not have the luxury of choice, Your Grace."

Exasperation clung to his voice. "Surely you have a preference. Many women of marriageable age have dreams of their future."

"As I am not married, I suspect that that is not an issue. Not all of us are dukes in need of an heir, Your Grace."

She was beyond appropriate. The conversation was scandalous, but Emmaline cared not. She could not have him, but she would speak her mind.

"You have just said you find the attentions of other men pleasing."

"I am well aware that my lack of dowry and status in society does little to recommend me, but I refuse to let that preclude me from enjoying a handsome gentleman's attentions. To do so would be folly."

"I believe you disregard their intentions too quickly, Miss Collins. Some men care not for dowries."

"Some, I am sure. But none of my acquaintance."

William's eyes pierced hers. In it she saw pain but steeled herself against any softer sentiment that sought to overwhelm her. She spoke only truth.

"You are correct in your observation, Miss Collins. I will need to marry. This is true." His expression *darkened and an inkling of unease shrouded her. "It is my duty."*

What was the meaning of this?

She did not wish to dwell on the bitter truth of her situation. He would marry. And from what she had observed with Lord Walcott, it would be an imminent betrothal to the worldly Lady Dewberry.

Not once in their dalliances had the Duke made any honorable offer to her. Not once since the day he had caught her in the greenhouse had he attempted to court her socially. There was no understanding between them other than that of carnal passion. She would not risk bruising her tender heart in the vain search of something more. Something that never could be.

Emmaline wished to enjoy her time left with William until he chose to announce his betrothal. She wanted desperately to forget about the way her heart was ripping in two at the thought of never seeing him again.

"If you would look not quite so pained, I may be able to procure another dance partner this evening, Your Grace."

"Another d—"

Emmaline received a perverse thrill at goading him. To witness the fire leap in his eyes, to enjoy the severe knitting together of his brow. Oh yes, she had him in a rousing passion. Her own, too, had been stirred. But what of it? What did it all mean?

It was her turn to frown. Nothing. Not a damned thing.

"A woman has needs just as a man."

William positively thundered, his movements stiff.

Emmaline continued, "Perhaps I might find even more . . . diversions in the country. I am, after all, unencumbered."

Oh, what a truly rousing passion he was in! She could see the battle in his eyes, the desire to keep his emotions in check, fighting against whatever baser desires burned between them. If they had been alone, she was in no doubt of what her punishment would be.

And Emmaline would take it and have her pleasure.

"Do not toy with me, Miss Collins."

"Or what, Your Grace?"

His jaw clenched. "Or . . ." He fought for restraint. "Or I shall prove to you just how powerful my needs are."

"The Season is almost—"

His voice was clipped, every word punctuated by desire. "The Season has not ended yet."

Emmaline felt the promise of his words burn through her dress, engulfing her body in a wicked heat. Oh yes, she knew what lurked beneath that restraint. How much she wished to unleash the wild, savage lover. To draw out his every desire until they were both left vulnerable and exposed.

But if Lord Walcott was accurate in his estimation, then William would very soon be claiming his duchess.

And come the end of the Season, she would return home.

Alone.

So Emmaline could not succumb to this melancholy. Would not. Long ago, she had vowed never to enter into a marriage devoid of love. Even if she received an offer from a gentleman, she did not think herself capable of accepting. Not now. Not when her heart belonged to William.

This Season, her relationship with Maddern had altered something within her.

So there was nothing left for a spinster to do but enjoy herself until the bitter end.

The problem was, the taste of bitterness was fast-approaching.

Chapter Four

Long ago, deep in the treacherous valleys and towering caves, there lived a beautiful dragon named Vanna. Her skin was dark as midnight, her scales as smooth as the lakes and streams by which she lived, high up in the mountains of Devil's Keep.

And every year, the villagers sent their own to defeat the dragon, win the gold, and save the fair maiden trapped by the dragon in its lair. Every year, the brave and valiant attempted to conquer the dragon, and every year, their bones lay deep in the rivers of Lake Eerlan.

As such, the kind but weary dragon lived her days, dreading the sound of man's footsteps, tired of the death, the destruction.

This year was no different. Vanna felt the change beginning beneath her scales. It was as imminent as the ever-changing moon, hanging heavy and portentous in the inky sky.

Not for the first time, the dragon with the skin as dark as night laid down her body in the echoey cavern of her lair and shed tears no soul but her own damned one could hear.

Arcas Delio of Three Waters heard.

It had woken him on the same day, a month from the full moon in the very blistering heat of summer, for three years now.

And every time he had heard the keening, heart-scrambling cry piercing his soul, he had ignored it, brushed it aside.

Except tonight.

Tonight, he awoke from his deep slumber, his body groaning in protest at the intrusion upon his dreams.

Easing himself from beneath the small, high breasts that muzzled him, Arcas rolled over and off of the fur-lined bed, making his way out of his keep.

While the woman had been comely, he had found the mating . . . wanting.

In fact, he had found many a thing wanting of late. For three years, if he were truly honest.

Arcas looked up at the grave-black sky and knew the time had come. Gathering what he needed from among his scarce possessions, he set out into the darkness.

He was not a man to shirk duty or responsibility

when action was needed. But this aching chasm he felt, this tethering of body to a different time or place, this something else needed to be explored.

He knew not what would come of it, but that did not matter. Arcas would chase it. Hunt it down, wrestle with it and himself until he emerged the victor.

Until he could recognize himself once more.

"What brings ye to these lonely parts?" The tavern was as full as expected on such a night, with wenches aplenty and locals feasting on game and stew. The tavern maid was a wry lass with a bony, lean appearance. No doubt the owner was cutting her pay and the lass had decided a hearty meal was a luxury she could do without.

"A journey."

He had travelled for three days, stopping only to sleep a little before moving on. Arcas had no sense of where he was headed but knew only to trust his instincts. And a restless urgency seemed to smother him any time he stopped for respite.

"Ye wouldn't be the first." She wiped at a particularly sticky substance on the bench, smearing the greasy stain further.

"And not the last, I am sure."

She crossed her arms, cocking a hip against the counter. "I suppose that whatever mysterious journey ye be on don't have nothin' to do with a dragon, now would it?"

Arcas' head whipped up. "A dragon?" Something inside of him shifted, as if a clear direct path through the fog made itself known.

"Aye, that got yer attention."

Arcas leaned forward, his tankard of ale forgotten. "What of the dragon?"

"As ye be not from around these parts, I believe it best to inform ye."

"So out with it!"

She grinned now, tapping at the counter. "That satchel looked mighty heavy when ye walked in. I might be able to help ye with that."

Arcas gritted his teeth. "Name your price." The itching, clawing need to know, the feeling that this was important, pressed between his shoulder blades, driving him to seek out answers. To act.

He placed a coin on the sticky bench. It disappeared before the candlelight gleamed across its surface.

"Well?"

"Her name is Vanna."

"The dragon?"

"Aye. And don't look so disbeliev'n. I've seen men come back from her cave, or whatever it's called, not the same as when they left."

Arcas bit back a retort. Such stories proved a fine distraction for wee ones from the hunger in their belly. But to think it real? To believe it true, the mythic, unconquerable dragon that frightened villagers? Arcas had seen too much bloodshed to believe it.

And yet . . .

"Go on."

"They say she is a fierce dragon, nigh unbeatable by common man. Legend has it that she stole one of the maids and kept her prisoner for hundreds of years."

"So the maid is two hundred years old?"

She frowned. "No. She be young and beautiful, with streams of dark hair and a sweet, sorrowful voice. The dragon has a spell on her to keep her such."

"Ye daft gurl!" came from a drunkard at the end of the counter. "'Tis not the maid who is cursed but the dragon!"

"I heard there is no maid!" cried another.

"I heard nobody returns," the tavern girl replied.

"Except for those whom you saw," Arcas pointed out, amused at the variation in such a legend.

"Ye can jest for all that's worth, but I know it be true."

A woman, old beyond time and bent with the heavy burden of it, hobbled up to them. She had a crescent-shaped mark on her left cheek, blue-black as if hanging from the edge of her black eyes. Her hair was a wild snowy white, with hints of red from the curls springing from every direction. When she looked up at him, he jerked, gripping the dagger at his waist, but stopped. Something snaked around his heart, giving him pause.

The woman's eyes became vacant. She opened her mouth, her voice low:

> "A valiant heart
> Hidden deep
> In the lair
> Of Devil's Keep.
> If love be sworn,
> If love be true,
> The curse once bound
> Shall break in two."

Arcas couldn't help but grin. A prophecy that rhymed. It must be true. He was about to tell the woman so when she spoke again.

> "You are the chosen
> What choice make you?"

Something beyond fear clutched at his bravado now. A warm heating of his blood, a pulsing, present *knowing* gripped him.

And in that moment he knew the old crone's words were true.

Genuinely, gut-wrenchingly true.

Arcas turned, taking a few deep gulps of his tankard, draining it.

"And have you seen this dragon . . ." He turned

back and then froze.

The woman was gone.

"Vanna," the maid replied, clearly thinking he had spoken to her. "Pay no mind to the ol' hag. The whole town knows she's crazy."

"Mmm."

Arcas paused, gazing at his cup, steadying himself. He did not spook easily, not after all the destruction he had seen. But this, the woman, her words, had shaken him.

"Have you seen Vanna?" he eventually replied.

"No. But sometimes at night, I hear the flapping of wings o'erhead."

"Has the dragon ever visited the town?"

"There were stories of—"

"Since your time, I meant."

She shifted, scowling. "No."

"And where can this dragon be found?"

"So you're after her gold then?"

"She has treasure?"

"Aye, lad, are ye daft? All dragons have treasure." The drunkard wiped the ale from his chin before stuffing the wedge of cheese in his mouth.

"And Vanna is said to be keeping a pure gold dragon's egg in her lair," the maid continued. "Some have tried to retrieve it, but none have succeeded. My friend came close once."

"And? What of it?"

"Well, he could not trick the dragon."

"Trick the dragon?"

"Aye, to get past her to the treasure. But the moon will be full soon and many will try it."

Arcas shook his head. Surely he was wasting his time?

But the old crone's prophecy echoed through his weary body, urging him to hope.

Arcas travelled for another five days and nights before he reached Devil's Keep.

Never had he believed the tale of a maiden trapped in the dragon's lair. Never had he followed the whispers of tavern maids and would-be warriors.

But as he stood there, at the base of Devil's Keep, Arcas felt the familiar shimmer of awareness crawling along his skin.

Dragons or no, the land was fucking creepy.

And exposed.

He stood solitary and vulnerable in a landscape that stretched out for miles east and west. There were no crags or valleys, no bushes or mountains to hide hunter from prey.

But there was a clear, worn path that shot out directly north, and before him, in the distance, sat high craggy rises and deep, dense boulders, formed with one message in mind.

For those unwelcome to fuck off.

Arcas had no death wish. At least, not at present,

but he knew as clear as his piss in the stream that this was the right way.

The only way.

Adjusting his pack, he continued on his journey. He would find his answers soon.

Chapter Five

Fantasy Core had rocketed her libido to greater heights that she wouldn't have thought possible. Every time she looked at Arcas, every time he spoke her name, the phantom of the Duke stood beside him.

Arcas and Maddern. Maddern and Arcas. One and the same.

So naturally, all Savannah wanted to do when they had a spare moment was fuck.

And funnily enough, so did Arcas. He was voracious in his appetite, aroused by the experience at Fantasy Core and wanting to screw her brains out whenever they had the chance.

Savannah stepped out of the shower, her long brown hair still damp, her nipples sensitive from the terry-cloth towel. And when she saw Arcas stretched out on the bed naked, she knew she couldn't resist him. From his devilish smirk, he knew it, too.

She strutted out stark naked and opened her sex

box. Rummaging through it, for it was almost brimming now with assorted items, she found the strap on dildo, nice and thick, then handed it to Arcas.

Next, she rummaged for the lube and grinned when she spotted the skin scratcher.

"Meow," Arcas murmured as she slipped two on her left hand.

Savannah watched as he put a generous amount of lube on the dildo, his hand palming the length in slow, sure strokes.

The teasing glint in his eyes was invitation enough. She crawled up to his chest, trailing the claw along his torso, loving the way his muscles clenched.

"I thought it was time we used this again."

"You don't see me complaining—fuck!"

She trailed it around his nipples, then went deeper at his abdomen.

God, he was glorious.

She would never tire of him. Never tire of the deep, sexy groan or the way he said her name.

Van. Savannah. Emmaline.

They were all embodiments of her. And he loved every one of them.

Wasn't she a lucky bitch to have that?

And she would lust and yearn after him, strong beneath her like this, enjoying it just as much as he.

Savannah continued scratching at him, shuddering when he tweaked at her nipples, taking one of the scratchers from her hand and tracing around her areola, then her nipple, making her grind against him.

Arcas trailed the scratcher up her thigh, hovering at her pussy, teasing her.

"Do it," she ordered. And when the rough edge glided up her labia, she jerked, heart thrumming in her chest.

Savannah wanted this. The next high. The next jolt. A bit of danger.

She took his hand, wrapping it around her throat, urging him to tighten his grip. And she ground against him, loving the pressure, the way her blood pumped as he squeezed.

She tapped at his hand when she was beginning to see stars.

"I want to take it further," Savannah gasped.

Arcas' eyebrows rose. "Than this? You want to try a restraint?"

"More."

"What did you have in mind?"

"A blade."

Arcas rubbed at his jaw, dotted with dark stubble. "Really?"

She pinched at her nipples, imagining it already. "I saw it at Orgy House."

"I know. I did too."

"And I bought a dagger, thinking we might use it."

Arcas's smile sent shivers across her naked flesh.

"I'm game. Yeah, I'm game. But you need to tell me your rules if you wanna do edgeplay right."

She contemplated it while she retrieved the silver dagger. Savannah explained what she wanted, that it was the element of danger and not bloodplay that she was after.

Arcas made sure he understood.

"So, no blood."

"Not a drop."

"Anything else?"

"Just not near my eyes or nose. But I'm up for a bit of mouth action. The movements need to be slow. Nothing too sudden or I might get jumpy."

"Noted." He stroked the back of her hand.

"And I don't want it in anywhere."

"Understood. No insertions, except for your mouth?"

"Yep. Happy to use my tongue, but not in my pussy or ass."

"Safe word?"

Savannah relaxed now, comfortable with the boundaries set. "The usual."

"'Wickham' it is."

Savannah grinned. "And you?"

Arcas thought about it, listing his requests. They were similar to her own.

Reassured, Savannah showed him the dagger. She smiled smugly when his eyes popped. It was not just any dagger, but one with a dragon-designed handle and sheath. The sheath was decorated in a robin-egg blue and stainless steel, the wings and body of the dragon carved in an intricate design.

She handed it to him before straddling his torso.

"It's gorgeous."

"Thought you'd like it."

"I fucking love it."

Arcas gripped the handle, admiring the head of the dragon and the imitation sapphire gem for its eye. He unsheathed the dagger, running a finger along the five-inch curved blade.

"You can play with it as much as you like. As long as you play with me too."

"Fucking A."

Savannah was turned on just watching him toy with the blade. His green eyes were bright, and she wasted no time.

Taking more lube, she ran it along the dildo strapped around his waist and lowered herself on to it, moaning at the pressure. She was stretched, a little nervous with this new element, but at the same time highly aroused. She adjusted herself, breathing out, rocking over his cock.

Savannah trailed the cat scratcher on his thumb and watched him shudder.

"I thought I was in charge here."

"In good time." She bounced now, using the claw to spark his arousal, watching as his expression turned dark and dangerous.

When his eyes rolled back in his head, she grinned, taking his thumb in her mouth. She sucked now, enjoying the sound of his pleasure, until the dagger hovered at her neck.

Her heart leapt, and after the initial jolt of fear, she felt the flooding of desire.

"I've been very naughty."

"How naughty?"

"I need to be taught a lesson."

Savannah rose up carefully, then down with great force, feeling the fear course through her at its sharp tip. It was a curved blade that hovered just at the base of her throat. She leaned forward, offering Arcas further access and delighted when he brought it to her mouth.

"Suck on it."

Savannah licked her lips, slowly gyrating against him. She rubbed at her clit then licked at the blunt end of the blade, until she reached the tip.

"Again."

Savannah shuddered, heart pummeling in her chest as her arousal built now. The pressure in her pussy, the danger of the dagger, all added to her experience.

She wanted more.

She licked along the edge, gasping at the sharp point, stilling as the steel clicked against her teeth.

"Yes," she breathed when Arcas trailed the dagger down her mouth and along her chest. The flat side of the blade circled around her areola, leaving a faint red mark. Arcas pressed the cold tip at her nipples, urging her to move.

And so she did, pumping his cock, working herself as the blade meandered over her body, pausing to press into her skin, flirting with the parameters she set for their play.

Never once did Arcas cross the line, as she knew he wouldn't. It was their deep trust that meant she could do this. Could know that he would stop if asked, that he would toy with her in the process, drawing out the danger—and her pleasure—because she asked. It made her desire for him limitless.

Arcas ran the edge up along her thigh to where her fingers flew over her clit.

"Move your hands."

She did, arching back so he had access there. Savannah watched, mesmerized as the silver dagger danced around her labia, teasing her clit. She rose up and down over him, drenching the dildo as the cold steel pressed against her pussy.

"I heard you need to be punished."

"Do I?"

"You've been a naughty slut."

"So bad. So . . . Fuck! Punish me, Cas."

He rapped the dagger against her thigh, sliding the blade along her flesh.

"Harder."

She felt the indentation of it on her skin and guided it back to the apex of her thighs. The winding pressure inside of her was building. The closer the dagger came to her pussy, the hotter it was.

But still, she wanted more.

They maneuvered themselves until Arcas was sitting up, his back against the wall. Savannah wasted no time in fucking him. Taking his free hand, she bit his thumb, hard, until he placed the blade at her throat.

"Yes," Savannah gasped. This was what she wanted.

The danger was what she lived for, here in his arms.

Arcas's eyes followed her mouth as she sucked at his thumb, working him until his head fell back.

"Van, you're so fucking hot."

"Are you close?"

"So. Fucking. Close."

She could see that he was. Knowing it, she sucked harder, using her tongue to swirl at the tip until he jerked and writhed, taking his fill.

She yelped when he gripped her hair, slowly easing her head back a few moments later, the dagger against her throat.

"Time to work that pussy."

Savannah didn't need any encouragement. She bounced on the dildo, working her clit with the sharp tip of the dagger at her throat. Her neck was exposed, and the pleasure-pain of Arcas' grip in her hair was enough to send the blood rushing through her. She rode him with abandon, every shift had the blade pressing farther in her neck, but she wouldn't stop. Couldn't.

And neither would he.

The glorious building began, and the force of it was so strong, she didn't dare hold back. It stole her breath, numbing her mind, and that swirling, pulsing, fucking glorious web of pleasure ensnared her body.

When she came, it was like nothing else.

Crying out, Savannah ground hard, shuddering in release, as if every inch of her body was an erogenous zone made for pleasure.

She slumped against Arcas, utterly spent. Then she sighed as his mouth lazily played with her nipples, licking and biting.

"As much as I love the idea of death by boobs, I think I have a few more decades in me yet."

Savannah grinned then shifted back, peeling off the cat claw.

"We can try that out next time."

Arcas kissed her, hard. "Game on."

Lying down now, they both curled into one another, Savannah's head on his chest, her body wonderfully sweaty and flushed.

She hummed as his hand traced patterns on her back.

"So how are you feeling being a regular at Fantasy Core, Your Grace?"

"Amazing, Miss Collins. You?"

"Same."

Arcas shifted to face her. "Out with it."

Savannah ran her tongue along the roof of her mouth before responding. "Was it odd coming out of it? Apart from the hungover bit, was it weird coming back to reality?"

"It was a shock, sure. One minute, I'm fucking your brains out, feeling my legs and my cock and everything else that came with it, then the next, I'm back to reality. So yeah, it was a jolt, but so is gaming for five hours and then having to take a business call."

"Good point." Savannah sighed, wriggling against him. "I can't stop thinking about it. Is that mad? Crazy?"

"This whole thing is wild, but it's not different from any other form of entertainment. It transports you for a moment, like your books, but you still know the difference between fiction and reality."

Savannah drew back, studying him. "Since when did you get so wise?"

"I'm like 200 years old now, remember?"

"Nerd."

"Given that we're checking in, you still cool with the whole monster fucking fantasy?"

"You mean kink? Hell yeah. Monster love me up, Cas. I can't wait to screw your brains out as a dragon. And just to clarify, you can never get too much kink."

He yanked her towards him, smacking her ass. "Fucking A."

Chapter Six

Sexcapades – The Edge of Desire

Holy choking mother of hell.

Edging is intense. Edging is raw. Edging is pain.

But fuck me, after my experiences at Fantasy Core (gotta try it–legit), I wanted something that pushed the boundaries.

The thrill. The excitement.

The fucking danger.

It wasn't just the choking, 'coz boyfriend has a tight grip.

It was the pure adrenaline of knowing that we were playing with real danger. Never in my life did I think edge-play was a kink I'd be into. But when he held that blade to my thigh, just on the inside, hovering near my pussy, I was gagging for it.

The way the tip of the blade pressed against my soft

skin until it met resistance, or a little deeper until it almost drew blood . . . Well, it made me want to come on the spot.

When it was at my throat . . . holy fucking hell, that was hot.

Would I do it with any Joe Blow I met on a sex app? Nope. No chance at all. Trust is an essential factor in edgeplay. But when it's with your boyfriend, and you know he gets off on you getting off, and you're just this big powerful throbbing ball of lust, hell, it's hotter than Hades.

Which I'm probably going to. But hey, gotta enjoy the ride, right?

A solid 8/10 on the O-meter.

Yours,

The Gamer's Girlfriend.

Dragons and dukes. The medieval and the magical. Savannah was wonderfully torn between being a dragon and fucking a duke and it was glorious.

New, exciting, an adventure she hadn't known she'd wanted.

Arcas was loving being the Duke. She was loving being the dragon. They were both exploring each other and enjoying the benefits of their real life and fantasy sex.

It left her humming as she shut the door of the apartment to go to her next library shift, happy in a way she hadn't felt in a long time.

But no sooner had she stepped onto the sidewalk than she froze.

"What do you want?"

The sickly dread that settled in her gut was an old familiar one.

Piers stepped forward, arms up. "I'm not here to cause trouble."

"Really?"

"I just want to talk to you."

"Talk. Indoctrinate. You don't know the difference."

"Savannah, I'm here because I care."

She shook her head, trying to remain calm. "Weren't the photos message enough?"

Piers' face transformed from confused to angered in a second.

"What are you blaming me for this time?"

Savannah turned and strode down the sidewalk, her brother trailing behind her.

"Hey, wait!" He tugged on her arm and she rounded on him, fury making her voice tremble.

"Don't. Touch. Me."

"What the fuck—"

"You don't get to stand there looking all righteous. You invaded my privacy, remember? I may not lead the lifestyle you approve of, but I don't appreciate being stalked."

"I don't—"

Savannah opened her satchel, taking out the folder of photos that had arrived just the previous day, and shoved it at his chest. She watched as her brother's face blanched at the images of her half-naked, clearly taken through her apartment window. There were more of her leaving Fantasy Core, some of her at the restaurant with Arcas . . . all invasions of her privacy.

"I didn't do this."

"Spare me."

His hands shook as he handed her the folder. Savannah studied his face, the one she had looked up to so often as a little girl, the one she had trusted to guide and protect her when she had been afraid. In it, she begrudgingly saw the truth.

"Then who the fuck did?" A slick fear coated the back of her throat, making it difficult to speak. "Are Mum and Dad having me followed again?"

"If they are, then it's for your own good."

"What kind of fucked-up answer is that?"

"Look, Savannah." He stayed close as she continued walking. "Mum and Dad love you. They're doing—we're all doing—what is best for your future. Your eternal salvation. You've rebelled, we get it. Now it's time to repent of your sins, to seek forgiveness."

"I don't need to repent anything."

"It's not too late to come back. Jesus loves you. Jesus will forgive you. You're ruining yourself for some selfish desire of the flesh, but you need to think about the future."

"My poor damned soul burning in hell."

"Exactly! The devil comes to steal, kill, and destroy. Look what he's doing to you."

Savannah almost laughed at the absurdity of it. And the fact that he had completely missed her sarcasm.

"Is this why you travelled all this way, Piers? Mum and Dad sent you to do their dirty work? Well, you can run back home like the good boy you are and tell them their heathen daughter isn't interested in returning to the fold like a lamb to the slaughter."

"So what?" he exploded. "You're just going to live like a whore? With your fucked-up boyfriend? Think of Mary Magdalene—even she turned from sin when she met Jesus. And he called seven demons from out of her."

"That is exactly why I don't believe your bullshit. Seven demons? Are you kidding me?"

"We can save you, don't you see? We're your family. We can give you another chance."

"I don't care about your version of redemption. I don't need what you offer. And before you go on, I have a family."

"What? With that gimp? Fuck, Savannah, he isn't a real man. He can never even give you children."

"Shut up! Just shut the fuck up!" Savannah heard the shrill tone in her voice. Even as the reasoned part of her cautioned herself against reacting, she couldn't help it.

She needed to assert herself, to make her stand against those who didn't respect her boundaries. Because to her, staying silent was akin to agreeing with them. She had stayed silent for too many years. She couldn't do it anymore.

Savannah continued, "I can't live the life you want for me. I don't want kids; I don't want a traditional family. I certainly don't want your fucked-up 'biblical' teachings. Don't you get it? Everything that I experienced while living at home has only brought me pain. I don't want any part of it. I don't want anything to do with you or your faith. All I want is for you to leave me alone. Stop the stalking. Stop the abusive texts. I mean it, Piers. If you really care for my soul, then leave me the fuck alone."

Savannah shoved the photos in her bag and fled. Her heart was hammering in her chest even as her brother hurled abuse at her back. It was only when she hopped on a tram that she felt like she could breathe.

Until she realized.

If Piers hadn't sent those pictures—who the fuck had?

Chapter Seven

*E*mmaline stood on the staircase of her aunt's home, gripping the balustrade. A pair of green, glittering eyes kept her captive, his gaze halting her descent.

William.

How could she hide all that she felt for him? How could she go on pretending that every look, every touch, did not sear her body, capture her heart?

For she was his now in every way imaginable.

Every way but one.

Fie! It would not do to think on it.

But with every dalliance, with every walk and picnic and play, she was fast becoming unable to contain her emotions. He unlocked the love she thought she had buried long ago.

And here she stood now, apart from and yet connected—in the most holy of ways—to this man.

William.

Willing herself to move, Emmaline descended.

"*Miss Collins.*"

"*W—Your Grace.*"

"*I am come to visit your uncle.*"

"*Oh.*"

She stepped closer, glancing to see there was no butler or maid to overhear. "*Why have you not come to me?*" she whispered.

William, too, stepped closer but answered quite matter-of-factly. "*I have been caught up in business. As you have in wedding plans, I hear.*"

"*How did you—*"

"*A duke knows all.*"

She breathed in, remembering the way his mouth had travelled over her. The way he had moved inside her, heavy and hard.

"*So I am led to believe.*"

A corner of his mouth twitched before he stepped back, his face unreadable. But in that moment, in that second, his eyes told her everything she needed to know.

Oh, how she longed for him! For even a minute more of his time.

"*Good day, Miss Collins.*"

"*Your Grace.*"

"*Ouch!*" Emmaline bit back a particularly lewd curse as the needle caught her finger.

"*Have a care, my dear, you are not a pincushion.*"

Emmaline scowled. She wished to throw her embroidery into the fire. She was in a temper ever since William's arrival. Lord, she craved movement, energy, excitement.

Him.

Whatever was taking them so long? What business did William have with her uncle?

She had been careful to listen out for his step but failed to hear it. With every passing minute, she was in agony.

"I am not a lady either." *She shoved aside her embroidery.* "My accomplishments are fair at best."

Her aunt crossed the room to sit beside her.

"You must not let him affect you so, my dear."

Emmaline stifled a gasp, swallowing it and the dread that circled around her chest. She did not know how to respond.

The Duchess patted her hand. "I have—"

Emmaline stood, gasping in surprise at the two individuals at the door.

"Mamma! Papa!"

"My dear girl." *Her mother beamed, brown eyes warming, even if tired from their journey.*

"Whatever are you doing in London? The wedding breakfast is not for a fortnight."

Emmaline rushed forward, embracing her parents, her embroidery joyfully discarded.

"Daughter, you look well."

"I am. I thank you, Papa."

Emmaline stepped back, allowing her aunt to welcome them.

"Ring for more tea, dear Emmaline. Your parents must be parched from their journey."

"It was not so tiring as expected, sister."

Her father harrumphed in protest. "Perhaps not for those of a stout constitution."

Her mother merely rolled her eyes.

"Come, Papa, sit." Emmaline beamed. "We shall have tea and you can tell me all about it." The heavy ache in her chest lightened. She missed them. Despite the wonders of London and the frenzy of the Season, seeing them here gave her a long-forgotten reminder of her home. A life that was simple, uncomplicated.

Uneventful.

Emmaline pressed her lips together. The thought surprised her. After all that had happened, she could not imagine returning to Wiltshire. No longer was she filled with a giddy expectation. She did not pine for the walk from the church towards home. She did not desire to lie on the green grass and watch the fat clouds roll away. She did not view home in the same fashion as she once had.

The very thought of returning left her feeling nauseated.

There was no life for her in Wiltshire. No future for her in London.

She did not fit.

Not now. Not after all she had sampled.

Emmaline tried to ignore the trembling in her

chest. She was lost. She could not stay with her aunt, trespassing on her kindness forever. Nor could she return home, back to a life devoid of fun and adventure.

Devoid of . . .

"I have come to seek support—"

William paused at the door.

"Your Grace. Allow me to introduce Mr. and Mrs. Collins, just arrived to attend their daughter's wedding."

Emmaline's heart seized. It was too much. She wished for a moment to digest what her aunt had been about to reveal, to bask in her parents' arrival.

But she was consumed by this new piece of information. What could William be seeking? What could require a private meeting with her uncle, to seek his support . . . for what?

But there—what was that? Why did her father barely acknowledge His Grace?

She watched in confusion as William's features shifted from eager to icy.

"We have met," *came William's stiff response.*

Emmaline's mother cleared her throat. "I have not seen you since you were a young boy. Is that not so, Mr. Collins? Why, it must have been a decade at least!"

"Indeed."

Emmaline felt it: the crawling dread, inching along her body, a sense that something was amiss.

"Papa?"

"Congratulations, Mr. Collins," *the Duke inter-*

posed. "It must be of great satisfaction to see your daughter engaged to a man such as Fanworth."

Her father bristled, discomfort radiating from him in palpable waves. "It is."

"A man of good fortune and breeding. Any father would be proud at such a match."

"I am."

"Mamma, Papa, His Grace was very attentive to Anne when she was ill. I am sure if it were not for the care he procured, she would have not quite so recovered."

"For that we are eternally thankful, Your Grace." Her mother smiled.

William inclined his head then stepped farther into the room. "Mr. Collins, I wonder if I could speak to you privately."

Emmaline glanced at William, trying her best to hide her surprise. This was very odd indeed.

Her father's mouth was compressed in a thin line. "I am afraid not."

"It would take but a moment."

Her father shook his head. "We have only just arrived. Perhaps another time, Your Grace."

"Very well. I take my leave." William's face was stony, his eyes distant.

He spared one last glance at her before swiftly exiting.

Gone was the soft-spoken lover who had looked upon her with tenderness, who had whispered to her in secret. Gone was the man who had lit her heart and body alight.

Emmaline whirled on her father. "Papa, what are you keeping from me?"

Henry Collins sat down, a closed, hard expression marking his features. "It is none of your concern, daughter."

"Perhaps you shall let me be the judge? Why would you refuse to speak with His Grace?"

"I dislike the Duke of Maddern."

"You do not know him."

"It was he who cried off when you last dallied with him, if you are so ready to forget?"

"I remember very well, Father."

"And in remembrance, I bid you to act with caution. He is not to be trusted. I thought we—"

"Yes?"

Mr Collins stood, shoulders stiff. "I am weary from the journey. I am in need of rest."

"Papa!"

"I do not forgive him for his ill conduct. If he has been showing his attentions to you, then daughter, I caution you. A man such as he would only want one thing from a poor spinster with little dowry."

There was a collective gasp around them.

Emmaline fought against the fury to speak, rising on shaking legs. "I may not be of marriageable age, Father, and I may not have received any suitable offers this Season, but I should like to think that I have the sense to know when I am being ill-treated."

"Emmaline, I did not—"

"I appreciate your concern, but it is not necessary. Come the end of the Season, I will return to Wiltshire. The Duke of Maddern and I will never see one another again."

She left, stifling a sob with her hands, tears blurring her vision.

How was it that her heart was full and yet breaking in two?

For the first time, Emmaline Collins wished she were a different sort of woman.

One with the means to make a man love her enough to stay.

Chapter Eight

"**D**early beloved, we are gathered here, in the sight of God . . ."

Emmaline did her best to keep her emotions close, but she found it unbearably difficult. There her sister stood, before the church altar, Lord Fanworth by her side. Anne's soft blue gown complemented her complexion. But perhaps it was the man she was marrying that caused her to glow in such a fashion.

Emmaline's eyes burned. Joy and an aching, bittersweet sadness threatened to overwhelm her. She would never experience this sacred ritual. She would never stand beside her betrothed making such a commitment. Love and honor. Duty and desire. A fallen woman now, with no offer to make her honest, she would forever be a spectator.

Of course she did not wish them ill. Her sister's happiness meant the world to her. In truth, she had feared Anne would find herself engaged to some lech-

erous toad with a grand fortune and a wandering eye. Instead, she had found a love match, and Emmaline could not be happier for her.

No, Emmaline's sorrow was entirely her own. She knew that all the joy and wonder she experienced in William's arms would come to an end. And soon. It was enough to make her do something rash.

What might her life have been had William chosen her all those years ago?

She dared to glance at His Grace, standing to the side of Lord Fanworth. Her heart leaped at seeing his green eyes watching her. Careful. Attentive.

Lord Fanworth's groomsman had been injured in a hunting accident and had been unable to make the trip. Apparently, Maddern had stumbled across his friend at the club, soused and feeling sorry for himself, and so he had agreed to stand up with him as his best man.

And yet, the Duke's presence only heightened her pain.

He was dramatically handsome in a dark coat, offsetting the white of his shirt. His green eyes were piercing and so very bright that Emmaline had difficulty tearing her gaze away. But it was in that expression, a warmth and tenderness, that stole her breath.

She only wished their circumstances could be different.

Emmaline glanced at her father's solemn face, his features pinched in discomfort. She tried her best to ignore his obvious disdain for the Duke, but her stomach churned at the discord between them. Indeed, William had attempted to engage him in conversation numerous times, but to no avail. Her father was not to be persuaded.

Emmaline had been acutely, painfully aware of it.

But once the ceremony concluded, and the feast had begun, it was as if she inhabited a stranger's body. All her senses were somehow diluted. The cold meats and delicacies were bland to the taste. The wedding cake, a wonderfully presented fruitcake, settled on her stomach like lead.

She was consumed by thoughts of William, by her father's warning of his intentions. That she was now a fallen woman was something she did not dwell on. She knew that Maddern's pursuit of her was exactly what she craved, but somewhere along the way, she yearned for more. In amidst the giddy exploration of her body, she had somehow given him her heart.

Emmaline glanced at her sister smiling serenely at her husband. She would not have this. Not with the Duke.

She did not believe William to be heartless. At the end of the Season, she was certain he would understand her refusal to continue their dalliance.

But where did that leave her? Once more caught in this uncertain state. She belonged neither to her old life nor to a dream of something new.

And the very thought of it made her weep.

"I had hoped I would find you here."

Maddern had followed her every move since the service. He noted the sorrow upon her face and wondered what had transpired since last he had seen her. When Emmaline had slipped outside, he took it as a fine opportunity to speak to her alone. Away from her father's scowling disapproval.

Seeing Mr. Collins brought back a raging anger he had thought gone. The wedding, the festivities, the merrymaking—none of it dulled the searing regret that pierced him at his actions long ago.

He was stupid to have dismissed what they shared back then. Even more foolish to have obeyed her father's orders to leave her be. He should have hunted her down and whisked her off to Gretna Green.

Tempting.

Still tempting.

But he had been duty bound then and, ashamedly, not man enough to back himself. He had been a marquess at the time, his father's sole heir, fresh out of Oxford. His father had threatened to disown him if he would not give Emmaline up, the daughter of an unremarkable, untitled nobody. He had threatened to give the Dukedom to a vile distant cousin, one who would ruin the fortune with his excessive gambling debts and penchant for liquor.

But what hurt the most, above all else, was that his father made him believe Emmaline did not care for him in return. That her friendly affection did not equate to love. His father had known that he had *wanted, more than anything, to find his equal. To seek out what his parents had never had in their marriage.*

A deep and everlasting love.

William had been torn between love and honor.

So he had said those hateful words, to sever their connection. And while they were not engaged, officially, they had had an understanding. The nature of their friendship was such that the natural next step would have been an announcement.

He had done what he had believed was right.

By the time he had realized his error, and plucked up the courage to make amends, her father had told him that she had moved on, that she was to be engaged —to the local vicar of all men.

His own eyes had confirmed it. Upon leaving Wiltshire, he had spotted her from his carriage, smiling up at a man who even at that moment had handed her a flower.

And that was when he had known. There had been no point. He had made his choice in the most unmanly, shameful way.

And he had learned his lesson well. He would not make such a grievous error again. He would not lose her a second time, out of a sense of duty, or social standing, or—

William watched Emmaline pace. She was breathtaking in white, soft and delicate and yet with a spine of steel he could only admire.

It was only when she turned to face him that he noted the despair. The deep, aching sorrow in her eyes.

"William!" she exclaimed.

"I cannot stay long, but I could not depart without seeing you."

"You risk too much! It is light. The guests and servants are everywhere."

I would risk it all, dear Emmaline, he thought for the thousandth time.

"Then I shall be quick," he said instead. Maddern reached for her hand, pulling her behind the hedgerows, even farther into the garden.

Wasting no time, he hauled her against him and feasted, taking her mouth in greedy, covetous gulps. His hands travelled along the line of her slender back and down to that round derriere. William gripped the soft flesh, wanting only to draw up her dress, to taste and touch her gloriously soft skin.

"You smell sweeter than any flower in this infernal garden. I cannot stand to meet in this fashion."

"Your Gr—William."

He pulled away, the blood pounding in his loins, his need an ever-hungry tiger ready to pounce.

"Come to Everton Hall."

Emmaline's mouth was red, her cheeks flushed. Her bosom rose and fell in an undulating wave. He was momentarily hypnotized, seized by the need to lay her on the grass and plunder. *No. He could not. Not here.*

"To your estate? I cannot—"

"I shall host a house party and invite your parents."

Emmaline shook her head. "My father would barely acknowledge your presence this morning. He will refuse your invitation."

William ground his teeth together. She was right. He had thought if he could at least speak to her father, initiate some polite conversation, he would have grounds to speak to him in private. But he would not be deterred.

"You are staying with your aunt and uncle. I shall invite them so that you can come."

"I am meant to return home once the Season is at an end."

"Delay. I beg of you."

He saw the battle in her eyes, the push and pull of her indecision.

Maddern lifted her palm, placing soft kisses to the tips of her fingers then trailing back down to her wrist. She sighed, mouth parting, eyes growing heavy.

"William." She trembled when he bit the pads of her fingertips. He heard her desire and only wished to extend it, to lose himself in her need for him.

"Yes?"

"I know—oh! What you . . . hmm . . . doing."

He gripped her close, swirling patterns on her neck with his tongue.

"I thought you might need some—" he groaned when she gripped his hips, dragging him closer—"persuading."

"Cad."

He grinned, trailing kisses on her face until he captured her lips once more.

"Is it working?" he murmured, pained by his need for her.

"Mmm."

Emmaline matched his passion with her own, and when her slender hand slid between them, stroking him through his breeches, he almost lost control.

"It is working very well indeed, Your Grace." She increased the pressure and Maddern pulled back, his blood pumping hot.

"Emmaline."

"William."

His eyes narrowed. Then he grinned. "Well played."

Amusement shone in her eyes. "You brought me here to seduce me into coming to Everton Hall."

"Yes. And imagine what I would do to you in the privacy of my home."

She shuddered. He could see the wicked thoughts flit across her face. A face which suddenly grew serious.

"But William, my father believes—"

"I care not for your father's beliefs. Do you wish to come?"

She bit her lip, staring back at him as if searching for an answer. After a time, she nodded. "Yes."

Maddern breathed a sigh of relief. "It is settled then. A fortnight. I shall organize for invitations to be sent." He *dragged her against him, holding her close. He gripped her hips, sighing as she wrapped her hands around him, running those delicate fingers through his hair.*

When she broke the kiss, whispering a scandalous suggestion in his ear, he shuddered. If he did not take his leave, he would do the very thing she suggested in the rose garden, in full view of the wedding party.

"Soon, sweet Emmaline." Maddern grinned. Very soon.

But first, he had a house party to plan.

Chapter Nine

Arcas, the fiercest warrior in all of Three Waters, was weary.

He was also filthy from the day's travels and wanted nothing more than to bathe in the cool, sweet waters that ran down from one of the many mountains in Devil's Keep. He was worse than a sty in summer and wished not to carry on so.

Dragons were wary creatures, and the mythical Vanna was no different. If he was to have any chance of stealing a look at her, of even crossing into the depths of her lair, then stealth was required. That, and a clear head.

For wasn't that why he'd heard the call?

For wasn't that why he was now here? Alone in the vast reaches of this treacherous terrain? One hoped he had not hazarded lava and lycans for naught. If there was gold, then he would find it, steal it, and be on his merry way.

For why else would he traverse all this way? He

was no thief, but if this dragon had stolen a maid, trapping her in the depths of its lair, then he would rescue the woman and take a jewel or two as payment.

A cooling swim and bath would be the ticket for this next stage.

It had been a bloody battle in Carthonal, and he had not paused for rest since then. Not much more than to fill his cup and seduce a wench for a tumble. The last lass had been bonny, he'd give her that. He smirked at the memory. He'd given her a lot more. She'd whimpered like an old crone plagued by the rheumy when he had left. And yet, still . . . there had been something wanting.

He put it down to preferring a fulsome woman. That the reason for this bereft feeling was not that there was something wanting inside of him, but that the lasses, while lovely, hadn't hit the mark.

He wondered if he needed a man. But if he wanted hard planes and raw rutting, he'd have fucked one of the endless men idling in farmhouses or bored after a bloody battle.

No, this calling ran deeper. Rubbing at the growth on his chin, he contemplated the journey before him and hoped a pot of gold rescued from the depths of a dragon's lair would be his cure.

She was stunning.

It was the only clear thought that sang through Arcas' mind upon actually seeing the dragon.

He had been wading in the cool clear lake, enjoying the dusk and the privacy of the trees, by which to bathe, when he had spotted a shadow in the distance. Startled, he had reached in his waistband and gripped his dagger, then simply gaped in awe as the form took shape. Its mighty, dark wings flapped slowly, gracefully, through the air. The dragon hovered above the lake, circling as if looking for the right spot to land.

Arcas had not moved, wanting to keep his place lest the dragon advance and burn his bollocks. He was also man enough to admit when he was afraid.

She was black and sleek, with wings long and shiny as the surface of the lake. Her eyes glowed a vibrant blue, almost unnatural in their hue. But it was the shimmering indigo beneath her scales that made her alluring.

He was spellbound by the flash, the glimpse of the underside of her scales as she smoothly entered the water, creating nary a ripple. Her movements were sensual as she frolicked in the water, oblivious to his presence. The small, sharp spikes on either side of her head ran down to her neck, giving way to a smooth, sleek body.

He had never seen a more radiant creature in all his life.

When he spotted the vast stretch of her wings, the

smooth shiny scales, as dark as the inky sky, his breathing slowed considerably.

And when those eyes turned to him, pinning him where he stood, he lost all breath. There was awareness there, in the tilt of her head, the almost knowing expression, as if she could read his thoughts.

"Exquisite."

For that she was. And no words or fanciful labels would ever do her justice.

Something stirred in his gut—a low, primal need. A whisper of it speared through his body.

Her ears were long and close to her head, fanning out towards her torso. And her tail, that long, wave-like ripple, swished and sashayed as she danced in the water. That was what it reminded him of: dancing.

Arcas stood before her, chest bare, dagger dangling from his loose grip, completely enthralled. If she chose, it would take just one lash of her tail and he would be incapacitated. She was fierce, strong, a warrior in her own right.

Arcas found it arousing.

The realization shocked him—at first. But then, he found he accepted it easily enough. The shock was not borne of abhorrence, but surprise. That it was as it was meant. As natural as the first time he had grown hair on his cock.

Arcas brought his hand up to wave, the dagger slicing up through the air only to land in the water with a plop.

The dragon flinched. Instantly, she was gone,

soaring into the sky with a powerful stroke of her wings.

"Wait!"

Arcas speared his hand through his hair, cursing at the missed opportunity. He did not move but watched her carefully as she tumbled and turned, yet another dance in the air.

Hands on hips, he watched her disappear towards the distant mountain peak.

When she was no longer in view, Arcas leant down, reaching in the water for his dagger. His semi-hard cock protested at the movement, straining upwards instead. Surprised, Arcas stared at it.

He should be focusing on finding the dragon, not pulling his poker. Nevertheless, he straightened then held himself, watching in fascination as his cock strained proud and hard towards the darkening sky. Without a thought, he pulled at his shaft. And that first contact, that heady rush of arousal that shot through him was exactly what he had needed.

Slowly now, as if in his own trance, Arcas palmed his cock in lazy strokes, up and down, stopping every now and then to swirl the pearly beads at his tip with his forefinger, coating his head.

He imagined touching the dragon, running his hands along her scales. Would it be cool to touch? Or as fiery as his need? He threw his head back, sinful images playing out behind his closed eyes.

Arcas' hips jerked, and he wanted to plunder, to take the mythical creature and bury himself inside of her until he could no longer see. He applied firmer pressure now, pumping his cock, craving the sweet friction, the ultimate release.

And when the driving need built up in his balls and the rushing sensation snaked along his spine, Arcas let go. His guttural cry echoed across the lake as silky hot ropes coated the cool blue water, carrying his desire with it.

Chapter Ten

Emmaline was heartbroken.

She was—oddly enough—also aroused.

Since her deflowering, her body acted of its own accord. It made its own needs known and did not care if it did so at inappropriate times.

Such as now.

Emmaline sat back in the carriage, determined to focus on her desire and not the whirling questions in her mind. William had made a point of inviting her aunt and uncle to Everton Hall so that she could attend. What did it mean? If it meant anything at all. Emmaline smoothed out her dress.

Because of the invitation, she had extended her stay—much to her aunt's delight—and promised her parents she would return home in a fortnight.

Even though their time together was rapidly drawing to an end, she refused to feel melancholic. This was her chance to enjoy herself, to indulge one final time in the sins of the flesh before parting ways from William. For good.

She stole a glance out the carriage window, admiring the impressive view that marked the Maddern ducal seat. While it was not her first trip to Everton Hall, it appeared so much more powerful now, so much more—commanding.

She gripped her hands, remembering the way Maddern had pressed his body against hers, the way his eyes had seduced her.

Emmaline shifted in the carriage, mindful of the wetness beneath her. She bit her lip, not at all ashamed. Only eager. So very, very eager for everything she could take from him. For all the memories she wished to create before they said goodbye.

When the carriage came to a halt, Emmaline sought to catch her breath. There, standing, waiting, was the Duke. William. She trembled as she waited for her aunt and uncle to alight first.

Maddern stood tall and proud and heart-wrenchingly handsome in a dark-blue coat, his pantaloons scandalously showcasing his strength.

If she were prone to swooning, she would do just that. Instead, she lifted her chin and stepped out of the carriage, meeting his warm gaze with her own.

"Miss Collins."

"Your Grace."

"I trust your journey was not too tiresome."

"Not at all."

"She has youth on her side," her aunt rejoindered good-naturedly.

William guided them through to the entrance hall.

"Perhaps I could give you a tour of the grounds after you have settled? I have made some improvements since your last visit."

Emmaline opened her mouth to refuse, but her aunt stepped in.

"I think it a delightful idea. Emmaline has a fondness for flowers and gardens. She has been a frequent visitor of our greenhouse this Season."

The quick light in the Duke's eyes was not to be missed, even if she were the only one to register its true meaning.

Emmaline felt the rising heat in her belly creeping up to her cheeks.

"Is that so? Perhaps I, too, shall have a greenhouse commissioned," the Duke answered. "I understand it is, after all, the latest fashion."

Emmaline lowered her voice, taking the opportunity while her aunt and uncle admired the entrance hall. "What game are you playing, Your Grace?"

"I should ask the same of you, Miss Collins. Tell me, how are your budding blooms?"

"None of your business," she hissed.

"Everything you do is my business." His eyes raked over her body. "Especially w—"

"Lady Dewberry! You are come as well? So very good to see you," she heard her aunt remark.

Emmaline jerked back from the Duke to see the lady in question descending from the staircase to greet them. While she had presumed Lady Dewberry would be in attendance, she did not expect her to already be here.

And as always, she looked immaculate. Her hair was perfectly coiffed. Her dress fell smoothly over her person, no wrinkles or creases from miles of travel—as though she had arrived days ago and settled in quite easily.

"Your Grace. Duchess. So wonderful to see you. Let me welcome you to Everton Hall."

Emmaline felt her claws curling, sharpening. How could that woman be standing there, looking so . . . so . . . . comfortable?

Lady Dewberry merely smiled. "Gill, be sure to tell Price to bring some refreshments to the Duke and Duchess of Carrington's rooms." Lady Dewberry smiled at the butler approaching Maddern.

Emmaline exchanged glances with her aunt. Who was she to assume the airs of the lady of the house? Who was she to order William's servants around so? A familiar unease settled in Emmaline's stomach.

It was exactly as Walcott had predicted.

She glanced at William, who even now seemed oblivious and was speaking to her uncle.

What had Maddern meant, to speak so intimately at her sister's wedding and now throw his betrothal to Lady Dewberry in her face?

She was horrified. Mortified. Crushed.

She started when Lady Dewberry approached. Linking arms, she guided Emmaline farther in the house and up the grand staircase.

"We must draw you a bath, Miss Collins. You look positively disheveled."

"I thank you for your kindness, but I believe I can arrange that with my maid."

Lady Dewberry smiled, patting her arm. "As a guest of Everton Hall, you must tell me if you are in need of anything."

Emmaline clenched her fists. It would certainly be frowned upon to maim another house guest, no matter how insufferable.

Pity.

Lady Dewberry continued, "Indeed, the Duke and I were speaking of it just before. I know you are a dear childhood friend of his and he has been most attentive to you. But as the Season is at an end, certain changes are to be expected. Once this party is over, I am sure we will not cross paths again."

Emmaline extricated her arm, turning to face Lady Dewberry as she opened the door to the guest room. Oh, how she wished to wipe that smug smile off her face. To tell her all the wicked things the Duke had been doing to his 'childhood friend.'

"I am certain you are correct," she replied serenely instead.

Lady Dewberry tittered. "Do you know, that is the very same thing the Duke tells me?"

"He prefers to be called William. At least, he prefers I call him that."

Lady Dewberry's mouth opened.

Emmaline smiled sweetly then curtseyed, closing the door on the woman's flushed face.

Chapter Eleven

Emmaline was torn. In one breath she was relaxed and calm, and in the next she was a hellcat in heat, ready to pounce.

The past week had been filled with excursions and picnics, card games and balls. The food was exceptional, the most succulent lamb, the sweetest fruit, all to be expected from the finest chef, an artist committed to nothing but the highest quality.

It seemed William's home, though grand, was tended by those who truly honored the people they served.

Even the well-being of his tenants, glimpsed on an outing to a neighboring estate, showed that the Duke of Maddern was attentive and kind and a man whom they all very much respected. In sum, Emmaline was moved by what she saw and did not wish to think that her time here would draw to a close.

More particularly, she did not wish to think her time with William would end.

Sampling her serving of fricassee one evening at dinner, Emmaline glanced at him, devastating in his evening attire. Every time she studied him, she was overcome by the image of his naked torso, muscles hard and heavy as he plundered her.

She resisted squirming in her seat, lest the other guests ask if she had some affliction.

Instead, she took a fortifying sip of wine, mindful of her bearings. This evening the Duke had invited a number of local families, and she dare not embarrass herself or bring scandal upon her family by acting out.

Especially as she was seated beside the local vicar.

"I must congratulate your family. Your sister's wedding in London, I hear, was the success of the Season," the vicar pressed when conversation lagged between them.

Emmaline nodded, swallowing her mouthful before turning towards the clergyman. He was a slight man, with owlish brown eyes and a warm, friendly disposition. If only she was not so distracted by another man, commanding and assured . . .

"Oh, yes. I thank you. It was."

"And are we to expect such happy news for yourself, Miss Collins?"

Emmaline placed her glass on the table, fearful that she would choke.

"I am afraid the Season has been unkind to Miss Collins," Lady Dewberry interrupted.

Emmaline bit her lip, stifling her gasp.

"I am without an offer," Emmaline finally concurred.

"But a house party at the end of the Season is the perfect place for matchmaking. Or so I have heard." The vicar gestured at the gentlemen littered around the table. Emmaline pretended to study the bachelors but knew that only one piqued her interest.

"I do believe," Lady Dewberry continued, "that you are correct. A house party always ends in an announcement. I am in no doubt such a happy event will occur."

The vicar's face was all smiles. Lady Dewberry was all saccharine sweetness.

"Is that so, Lady Dewberry?" Emmaline questioned. How she wished to flick away that smug smile off—

"It is, indeed, Miss Collins."

"I have not heard such happy news."

"I am not surprised, my dear. You see, we run in different circles."

"I must admit I am also in the dark," the vicar interrupted, obviously seeking to support his dinner companion. "But a betrothal is a happy occasion. Two people in the sight of God, making a sacred commitment to share their lives together . . . It warms my heart to hear it."

Emmaline nodded, Lord Walcott's comment still circling in her brain. If what Lady Dewberry hinted was correct, that her engagement to the Duke was soon to be announced, then Emmaline had less than a week to prepare herself for the news.

And her departure from the Duke's home.

"Oh, and Miss Collins, I must commend your modiste for your gown. It is truly . . . befitting."

Emmaline gritted her teeth.

It would be a shame to ruin a beautiful muslin gown, but Lady Dewberry's insufferable reply might just warrant it.

She smiled to herself then froze, locking eyes with the Duke.

Whatever was she supposed to do now?

She would seek her pleasure. That was what she would do.

Emmaline made the decision once the ladies retired to the drawing room. The gentlemen had parted some time earlier for port and brandy, but even the most scandalous end of Season gossip could not hold her attention. Once the guests broke up for tea and cards, Emmaline would take her leave.

She had imbibed to the full this evening, and the loose, giddy sensation that stole across her body only seemed to heighten her ardor. She wanted Maddern's mouth between her thighs. She longed to feel his cock stretching and plundering inside of her.

Emmaline all but trembled from the force of it. She allowed her imagination full reign, shifting at the tell-

tale dampening between her thighs. When tea was served, she rose and on unsteady legs, slipped out of the stuffy room. She took a fortifying breath as she entered the hall then wandered down the corridor. Where would she find him?

When she heard laughter behind William's study door, she knew she had found her mark. Glancing around her—at the blessedly empty corridor—she grasped the handle, turning it deliberately.

"I thought I might find you here," she said, her eyes pinned to William as she stepped inside the room.

But he was not alone.

There, Walcott lounged opposite her lover, his feet propped on the mahogany card table anchored between them. Walcott scrambled to stand, to acknowledge the presence of a lady.

Emmaline waved him aside, a new, wicked idea forming in her mind.

Driven by drink and excessive spirits, she locked the door and sauntered towards them both. William's cravat was undone, his hair slightly mussed, and his wicked mouth—the very same one that brought her to rapture—curled questioningly at the edges. She wished to trace her finger along the line of his jaw, to feast on the throbbing pulse at his neck. Her own breathing turned shallow.

Oh, how she needed him. So very desperately.

"Miss Collins?"

"Your Grace."

She lifted her skirts, emboldened by her sudden

plan, then straddled him, lowering herself down. His hands shot out to grip her bottom. Surprise stole across his face.

"Perhaps I should take my leave?" drawled Walcott.

Emmaline glanced at him over her shoulder. "Stay, if you please. What I have in mind concerns you, too."

Walcott raised his eyebrow. "I am ever eager to please."

Emmaline turned back to watch William, his eyes suddenly intense.

"What have you in mind?"

"I thought that was obvious." She took his hand, placing it under her dress. "I want you."

"And Walcott."

"I wish to . . . expand my education. You share many things."

Maddern's jaw tensed. He gripped her thighs. "And you wish to be one of them?"

Emmaline shrugged. "Yes. I thought you would teach me something new, something wicked."

Walcott laughed. "Very well done, Miss Collins. You have come to the right place."

Maddern brought her closer. "I see I have corrupted you soundly."

"Is this a problem?"

"Not at all." William stood, placing her on the edge of the table, cards scattering. "But know this," he murmured as he stroked her beneath her dress. "You

are my lover, is that clear? When all the fun and games
are over . . . you are mine."

Emmaline smiled indulgently. "I thought you
liked sharing."

He stroked her harder. "To a point."

"Oh! There." Emmaline rocked against him, shuddering at the pressure.

"You will drive me to ruin," Maddern murmured
before kissing her, stroking her, filling every need inside of her.

He bent his head, hovering at her collarbone, in-
haling deeply against her skin, all the way up her neck
to her temple.

Emmaline shivered, heat curling low in her belly.

She had but a moment to draw breath when Maddern crouched before her, his mouth traveling up her
legs, finding the soft flesh of her thigh before unrav-
eling her with his tongue.

She gasped, steadying herself on the edge of the vel-
vet-covered table.

Emmaline turned, inviting Walcott over. "Kiss me,
Lord Walcott," she commanded. He approached, cupping her face, a wicked light in his eyes.

Walcott's mouth was firm and yet gentle. He
teased with short samples, then in drugging drawn-out
kisses. Below, William's hands gripped her thighs. His
mouth was a frenzy over her heated flesh. He found the
part of her that couldn't be contained, and he wasted
no time in sending her hurtling into pleasure.

"Yes." She was breathless, unable to catch air, dizzy with the thrill. "Yes."

Walcott toyed with her breasts, aching and heavy in her gown. He tugged down the fabric, feasting on what little flesh he could access.

Dear God, it was heaven.

She bucked as William's rhythmic licking only increased in intensity.

Lord Walcott's raspy growth grazed her cheek. He drew her forward, off the table, to properly undress her. His fingers were competent and quick, better than any lady's maid and far more dangerous.

Maddern hovered beneath her skirts, his hands still gripping her thighs, but his mouth did not move over her. She whimpered from the absence.

She recalled Walcott's tupping of the woman at the Cyprian ball and could not contain her need.

"Maddern, please." She panted when her dress began to give way. Walcott kneaded her breasts, and she leaned back against his hard chest, succumbing to his surprisingly rough and calloused palms.

He unpinned the front bib of her dress, dragging it down to her stomach, nails trailing down her chest. She felt the tell-tale hardness at her bottom and moaned. What would he be like? Would it feel the same? She had only ever lain with the Duke, but now another was waiting, the rhythmic knocking at her back signaling his arousal. And she wanted it all.

The squeezing pressure at her breasts and Maddern's persistent tongue, now firmly affixed on her, was *too much. Gripping William's shoulders, she followed the rising orgasm that washed over her, knees buckling. She shuddered, held upright by both men until she slumped back against Walcott, legs shaking.*

The Duke emerged seconds later, eyes wicked. A satisfied smirk sat upon his face, but she was too sated to care. The man had a silver tongue after all.

Limbs wonderfully heavy, Emmaline allowed Walcott to finish undressing her. He picked her up and carried her over to the rug in front of the fire. Laying her down gently, he stretched out beside her, stroking and caressing her bare flesh.

His hands wandered over her body, appearing aimless but for the expression on his face. His dark eyes watched her reaction, hovering over the dip behind her knees or the underside of her breast, seeming to make a note of her responses.

He was careful and gentle but no less potent than the man that sat at the foot of the fireplace, watching wordlessly.

When she reached for Walcott's breeches, he quirked a brow then moaned at the contact.

Lord Walcott kneeled, stripping away his clothes with greater speed. He was not as thick as the Duke, but what he lacked in girth he made up for in length.

Emmaline pressed him down to the ground then kneeled above him. There was something so very wicked about touching another man in front of William. It made her feel wonderfully bold and brazen.

Lowering herself, she began to pleasure Walcott, first with her fingers then her mouth, just as the Duke had shown her. Walcott gripped her hair, guiding her, adjusting the pace.

She shivered at the fingers trailing down her back.

A cool breeze whispered along her calves and up her thighs as the Duke approached behind her. She positioned herself on all fours, breasts swaying as she lapped at Walcott's hard cock.

Maddern toyed with her, fingers beckoning, setting a pace that her rocking hips met with eager abandon. She was aware of Lord Walcott's groans through the veil of her own arousal. When Maddern pressed against her, naked and heavy, she paused. He gripped her hips, adjusting his weight and the angle of her body before easing into her.

Emmaline shuddered then increased the pace, working Walcott with her mouth, enjoying the murmurs from the man behind her, one who seemed to shed any reserve when in the throes of his own passion.

"Emmaline," William muttered, leaning against her back, burying himself even deeper inside her. The heat of his body, the whispered words of encouragement surrounded her.

She struggled to draw breath. Her mouth was full, her body wonderfully worshipped, and the pleasure, insistent and pulsing deep inside, rendered her incapable of thought.

Good heavens, that this could be so good!

She drew back from Walcott, seeking to take him

deeper, but William shifted her to an upright position. In seconds, she was again caught, sandwiched between two hard planes. Walcott claimed her mouth, crushing her nipples against his chest, while William continued to plunder her.

She broke away, panting, only to have Walcott's mouth on her breasts, nuzzling and biting.

"Please, I need . . ."

"Not yet," Maddern commanded, withdrawing from her completely.

A nod between the two men, and Walcott lay beneath her once more, wasting no time as he positioned her above so that she straddled him. He thrust inside her before she could draw breath to finish speaking.

Emmaline gasped. The angle of it, the easy access to the soft, swollen part of her, heightened every aspect of the carnal act. She bounced over Walcott, adjusting to the variation in length and girth, marveling at the way he felt. When his fingers found the quivering spot, she closed her eyes in abandon, rocking over him, flushed and shaking.

"Are you ready for your duke?" Maddern questioned.

She frowned as William hovered behind her then gasped as he pressed her torso down, so that her breasts were crushed against Walcott's firm chest.

"William?"

He ignored her questioning. Instead, his fingers trailed along the path of her bottom, hovering at the point where Walcott was thrusting inside of her. She gasped as his finger slid inside.

"William!" Emmaline jerked.

Walcott held her chin, their faces close. "We shall take turns," proffered his lordship. "One thrusts in, the other out, stretching you until you have us both."

She couldn't control the trembling in her body. Both men at the same time. Merciful heavens! It was beyond what even she had imagined!

With slow strokes, William's fingers stretched her, sliding and adjusting until she grew accustomed to the feeling.

Then she felt the moment when Maddern replaced his fingers with his cock. She gasped at the intrusion, a stretching, pulling sensation as he slowly entered behind her. William took his time, murmuring words of encouragement as she relaxed her muscles. He was thick and hard, demanding entry. And by slow degrees, they found a new rhythm. She liked this angle, the feeling of his heavy balls slapping against her. It was primitive and base, making her feel naughtier for craving it.

Emmaline shuddered, the pressure great, the sensation, after some time, exquisite.

She was stretched and filled, so completely full, she had no words for the wonder of it. She panted, drawing in as much air as she could. Was it possible to faint from pleasure? From the winding, tightening need that coiled inside of her?

Both men thrust in and out in a syncopated

rhythm. She could barely breathe from the wicked sensations.

"Yes . . . Oh, yes," she whispered.

Every shift and sigh, every stroke and murmur were magnified now.

Walcott took her mouth, stroking and teasing, building her need. Her limbs trembled from the pressure, the sheer fullness of being trapped between them.

Emmaline groaned, feeling the building in her body, rubbing against the man beneath her, hitting the soft spot that drove her beyond reason.

The rolling, aching pleasure continued its ascent until she was blind to all else except the point of contact between her thighs. The slapping, grinding of the men within her captivated her, so that she was both aware of all the sensations, the heat of the fire, the friction and sweat, but also hovering just outside herself.

"This is . . . I don't—" She sobbed William's name, unable to control herself. She trembled then shook as her body strove for fulfilment. She climbed higher, cresting at the peak then rapidly falling off the edge, tumbling, flying, spinning out of control. She begged, pleaded, cried out as the power of her release pounded through her, the men doing the same until she was coated, her bottom and belly sticky with their seed.

Emmaline was lost, delirious, in a state of abandon and bliss. The heavy presence of the two men, the lightness of her mind and body, was wondrous and heady. It was a wonderful, wicked new exploration to add to her lessons with William.

She only wished they had done it sooner.

All three slumped on the carpet, chests heaving, bodies spent, not one of them moving. Emmaline was not certain they ever could.

"She will make a fine duchess, Maddern," Walcott murmured.

His Grace grunted in response. "That she will."

Chapter Twelve

I t wasn't like in the movies.

That was Savannah's first thought upon being kidnapped. The sheer speed of it stunned her. She was ashamed to admit that her first response was to freeze. Her whole body was locked in tension, the fear gripping her throat, silencing her better than any gag or gun could.

"What the fuck?" she spluttered, sprawled in the back seat.

One minute she had been walking down the sidewalk, mere meters from home, and the next she was tackled by two men into an unassuming looking SUV.

The moment she had looked up at Arcas, waiting outside of their apartment in a snappy suit for date night, was the moment she had had the wind knocked out of her.

Savannah shuffled around in her seat, heart thumping. She managed to catch a glimpse of Arcas, arms moving like pistons on the wheels of his chair as he chased after her. Terror seized her body, numbing her ability to respond. She watched helplessly as the distance between them grew. The driver took a sharp left turn and Savannah's head smacked against the windowsill.

And all went black.

When Savannah came around later, her movements slow and stiff, the winding jerking motion of the vehicle had vanished. Instead, she looked up to see them racing along the highway, a blur of cars rushing past.

She stifled a hysterical laugh, looking behind her. She almost expected the police to be giving chase with Arcas beside them in the passenger seat. All she could see were men and women driving their own cars, minding their own business.

And then she looked up, her lungs seizing.

"Leo!"

She hadn't seen him in years. The sandy blond hair he once wore spikey was now shaved. He sported a bushy beard that made him look older, more mature. Gone was the lanky teenager she had once known. He was heavier now, and from the wild look in his eyes, not at all well.

Savannah glanced at the man in the driver's seat. He looked vaguely familiar, but she couldn't place him. How did he know Leo? Her mind began conjuring scenarios that made her stomach clench in anxiety. She was at the mercy of two men, trapped, with no way of seeking help.

Everything she had read about abductions told her that it was best to fight, to stop them from taking you to another location. Because once they did, it was over.

Panic, the heavy, suffocating terror of it, seized her now. *Breathe, Savannah. For fuck's sake, you need to think.*

With every breath, she pictured Arcas encouraging her, giving her strength.

What the fuck was going on?

Why after all these years?

Savannah gasped, her mind frantically piecing the jagged edges together. "It was you!"

Leo smiled, but the expression was cold, his smirk oddly terrifying.

"I wondered how long it would take for you to realize, but you just didn't fucking get it."

"Why?" Savannah gripped the straps of the seat belt.

He looked her over. Even with her jacket on, Savannah felt violated. It was a leering inspection, one that spoke of a twisted desire. Never once during her sex work online had she felt disgusted, but one look from Leo and she wanted to scrub her skin raw.

There was something not right about him.

"Why? You owe me."

"Owe you? That's why you've been stalking me? Sending me pictures? Because I owe you?"

"I've seen your channel. Spreading your legs to every man like some whore. Your man can't take care of your needs, and you need someone who can. I was patient all those years, respectful that you wanted to wait, that you weren't ready. But then you went off to college, fucking around like some slut. I heard your mamma confessing to mine of your wicked ways. And I knew, I knew you owed me what you didn't give me back then."

"What the hell?"

"You're MINE!" Leo roared, spit flying.

Savannah flinched, pressing against the car's leather upholstery.

"Easy, man."

"Shut up, Simon. Shut your fucking mouth!" Leo pointed the gun at him.

"Okay, fuck's sake."

"I don't owe you anything." Savannah glanced at the turn off, one she remembered from long ago. "Wait, where are we going?"

"You'll see," Leo muttered.

"Are we heading back to Bellingham?"

"Not just a pretty face, are you?"

It was starting to get dark, but as the sun was setting, Savannah knew she had to figure something out. She knew the road ahead, the turn off, the dual carriageway that would be replaced by a single two-lane road. Then lay the straight stretch of bitumen leading to the one place she never wanted to return to. The one place that had never truly been home.

The closer they got the Bellingham, the harder it would be to escape.

"I just want to understand," Savannah said, keeping the fear, the disgust, out of her voice.

"I thought I was clear."

"What do I owe you?"

"Marriage."

Savannah spluttered. "What?"

"We had an agreement, your parents and mine. We were meant for one another. I thought by letting you go that you would see what you were missing. Instead, you got corrupted. College made you a whore. But I can make you whole again. You can come back to the church. Come back to your community."

"Come back to you?"

"I've spoken to Piers and your parents. I have their blessing."

"Their blessing?" Savannah watched his anger dissipate. A smug expression tugged at his eyes and mouth. "You spoke to my parents?"

"I did it the right way. Not like that pathetic guy you live with, corrupting your soul. I told your parents I still want to marry you. I'm forgiving you your sins just like Jesus would. And those in the community will forgive you, too, once you're my wife. Simon's old man, Pastor Rick, is gonna be the ticket to your salvation. My buddy here is going to help me make it happen."

Savannah kept her breathing even. Hysteria would not do, but the same helplessness assailed her. The very same sense that she was being violated, that she was powerless, resurfaced. It was the same pain she had felt all those years ago while being abused. The very same twisting in her gut as rage and anxiety and fear threatened to seize her body. Her hands trembled. Savannah shoved them in her pockets, freezing when one grasped her tube of lipstick. She clutched it, her lifeline to Arcas and their date night.

"Leo, we've both changed. I haven't seen you in six years. What makes you think we're compatible?"

He scratched at his chin with the gun as if considering. "The man is the head of the household. It is through his dictates that the woman must abide. When I lead you to the path of holiness, you'll be renewed. Trust in me, Savannah. Trust that I can make you good again."

Savannah wanted to fight, to tell him he was sick and disgusting and fucking crazy, but she bit her tongue instead. And tasted blood. She needed to make him believe she accepted his plan. She needed to buy herself some time to fucking come up with her own.

"Teach me more."

Leo shifted again, studying her face before finally conceding. "Okay then."

He settled in. The dry countryside of Victoria sped past. He spoke of scriptures, of the future they would share. All Savannah could think of was a way out. She nodded, asking the right questions, seeking to draw him out.

"So when will we marry?"

"Tonight."

Savannah's eyes popped. "Where?"

"In Bellingham. In our church. In *your* church."

Never her church, Savannah wanted to shout, but she stayed silent, desperately trying to school her features. Though it felt like wearing a straitjacket, her eyes stayed on his gun. Leo—even the old Leo she remembered from her childhood—was odd and unpredictable. She had no wish to die.

When the signs for Bellingham grew closer, Savannah's heart thumped. The land stretched out on either side, dark and distant. Gone were the buildings and farm stays. All that she could see was the dark countryside and the ever-increasing remoteness.

It stretched before her like some gaping chasm.

Who would save her? This wasn't some crime novel, but real life. Her life. Maybe if they stopped somewhere, she could plead with someone for help. Maybe she could run?

Savannah looked down at her heels. Not exactly getaway gear. Fuck. She was dressed for a night out with Arcas, some dinner and cocktails. Maybe a late-night walk.

And then the thought pounced on her.

"Husband, could I make a small request?"

"You can."

"I'm hungry and thirsty and well, I need to . . . relieve myself." She took a deep breath, trying to ingratiate herself, to use her very real fear to appear meek. "Could we perhaps take a break at the next service stop?"

Leo was silent for some time.

"C'mon, man, I'm starving. Let's get some Mexican or something," Simon cajoled. "Think of it as your bachelor party."

Leo glanced out in the distance then looked at Savannah. "Remember, I'll have my gun in my jacket. So if you think you'll run, think again."

Savannah smiled at him reassuringly, gripping the lipstick tube in her pocket even tighter. She was helpless without her phone and purse, but she couldn't focus on that.

She didn't dare lose hope.

Chapter Thirteen

William spotted Emmaline beneath the ash tree as he returned home from an early-morning ride. She had her face tilted up to the sky, the drizzling rain kissing her glowing cheeks.

He turned immediately.

Their lovemaking, the wonderfully wicked shared experience the evening prior, lingered in his heart. She had been eager and open and utterly beguiling in the firelight.

And now she was here, in a place he could see her all alone, albeit if only for a short length of time.

Stirred, Maddern galloped towards her. Reins in hand, one leg crossing over to dismount, he was about to hail her with a teasing comment when he noticed the tears streaming down her cheeks.

Instead, he stopped, dismounting sharply.

The movement startled her—instantly she turned to dash away her tears. His heart twisted painfully.

Maddern strode towards her, gathering her close.

"What is it, Emmaline? Tell me."

Her wracking sobs pierced his soul. A woman's tears were a source of great discomfort, but to have Emmaline so distraught in his arms was akin to torture.

She shook her head, burying close.

When the light rain turned heavy, he pulled her beneath the branches of the tree to take cover under what little shelter it provided.

"What is it?" He blinked away the rain, holding her face.

She was unchaperoned, far from the house, and in great distress. All William wanted to do was wrap her in his arms and shield her from the pain.

What he felt for her had shifted.

No, not shifted, for it had always been there. But now, it was not something he could dismiss. It was not something he ever wished to deny either.

"Is it your sister?"

She shook her head, looking up at him with such sorrow, he had to close his eyes momentarily against the pain.

"Your parents?"

She wrenched away from him, pacing in the torrential rain, the heartache and pain she felt as heavy and grey as the storm clouds above.

William rubbed at his chin, casting off his riding coat. "At least take this." He brought it around her shoulders, holding her in place. "What is it that has made you cry?"

"Please, Your Grace. It was a private moment, not one I wish to share."

William's eyebrows rose in surprise. "We are alone. There is no need for formalities."

"I disagree. At the end of this week, I shall return home and you will remain here. I think it best that we prepare ourselves for the shift in circumstances now. Do you not agree?"

Maddern frowned. "Shift in ci—"

"Our arrangement will come to an end and I . . ." Emmaline looked away. "I shall never see you again." Her eyes filled, and she titled her face up to the sky as if to wash away the tears.

"Emmaline!" He gripped her shoulders, fearful. "This is not the end."

She shoved at the strands of hair now matted to her face. "Of course it is. And it pains me." Her lip wobbled. "Damn you, William, for doing this to me!"

Maddern rubbed at his chin, aroused and shocked at her language. But he wished not to be blinded by it. Not yet.

"If I am to be damned, then I will take you with me."

William yanked her against him, capturing her reddened lips in a searing kiss. His heart throbbed, his body yearned, but what he felt surpassed the physical.

"You care for me."

"I do n—"

"As I care for you."

Her breathing hitched as she looked up at him, trembling.

"And I do not wish for this to be over."

"But it must, Your Grace."

"Stop calling me that!"

"It must! We live separate lives. Nothing has changed. I am still a poor spinster—"

"Hellfire! You are mine."

"For how long, William?" She twisted out of his arms. Discarding the coat on her shoulders, she began to pace. "You are cruel to toy with me, saying I will make a fine duchess. I am a fallen woman without any other prospects. What will you do when you tire of me?"

"Tire of y—Confound it, woman!"

"You will leave me as you did long ago."

The verbal slap was as powerful as any blow.

"Emmaline . . ."

"You severed any chance at a future ten years ago. Not once did you think to write. To visit. Our dalliances now are of a private nature. Not once have you made your feelings public. Not once have you shown a desire to court me. So it is very right for me to say that we must end this arrangement now."

William ground his teeth together, pained by her confession.

No, this could not be. He needed more time to make it right. To make amends for the past.

"You are mistaken."

"You made a choice, as you did long ago. And now I am making mine. Come the end of this week, we are strangers."

"I did see you."

Emmaline crossed her arms, bosom heaving. "I beg your pardon?"

Maddern shook his head. He should have known. He should have known that she was none the wiser, but he had no one to blame but himself.

"I visited. I was fresh out of Oxford and sick at the thought of how we parted. I came to Wiltshire. I came to see you."

Emmaline's mouth opened.

"Your father was at home. I told him of my desire to renounce my title, give up my fortune, for a chance at courtship with you."

Emmaline's eyes filled anew. Her hand, delicate and trembling, hovered at her lips.

William continued, but the pain was like a fresh wound, one he would not staunch.

"I stupidly believed my own father's lies: that you did not care for me, that what we shared could not sustain us. But with every passing month, I knew I had made a grave error. I felt sick at the thought of never seeing you again."

"But what did my father say when you visited?"

"That I did not deserve you for treating you so ill. That an honorable man would have chosen you at the first—over rank, over title, over fortune—and that it *was best that I leave and never contact you again. That you had begun to smile once more, and he wished not to see you in pain. That I would be nothing without my title and wealth, and that you deserved a man to give you a comfortable life. In short, a match between us would never work because he had experienced the worst of society in daring to marry your mother, a titled woman."*

"Oh . . ."

"I am ashamed to admit that I listened. I did not wish to cause you any further pain. I saw you on my way out, smiling as he had said, and instead of beating the brains out of whomever it was you were smiling at, I stole away, thinking it for the best."

"Oh, William." Fresh tears fell as she stared back at him.

He was not ashamed to realize it was not solely the rain that blurred his vision.

"Forgive me, sweet Emmaline. Forgive me."

She rushed at him, drawing him close. William held on, wrapping his arms around her waist, moaning when her mouth fused to his. She was everything he yearned for, soft and sweet and achingly tender. Like the rain, her kisses washed away his sins.

In her arms, he found life. In her arms, he felt peace.

"I forgive you." It was a silent murmur in his ear. A quiet offering, the sweetest of gestures. "But this does not change our circumstances."

"*To hell with circumstances.*"

Because in Emmaline's arms—he had been proven wrong.

In Emmaline's arms—he found love.

Chapter Fourteen

The roadside diner had the usual odd assortment of fast-food options. Savannah smelled the sharp tang of onions mixed with aromatic Italian herbs, fried burgers, and spicy curries.

Her stomach rolled in disgust.

As they walked past people tucking into their burritos or pizzas, Savannah tried to catch someone's eye. But everyone was busy with their meal or slumped over in booths, taking the opportunity to sleep before hitting the road.

"Let me freshen up first?" Savannah swallowed.

Leo shot her a hard stare.

"I'll take her." Simon grabbed her by the arm.

Leo opened his mouth but closed it again. "Be quick."

Savannah walked down the back of the diner, to where the restrooms were located, then jerked when Simon followed her inside.

"What are you doing?"

"You can go and I'll just wait here."

She pressed her lips together. The windows above didn't offer any chance to escape, but she didn't like him waiting so close.

Savannah checked the first stall, but it was out of paper. She walked out of it and into the second, pretending the first had been too dirty. And—thank Jesus —there was paper there.

She slowly sat on the seat, trying to even out her breathing.

Savannah wound down the few strips of toilet paper with shaking hands. Taking out her lipstick, she wrote an SOS note requesting that they call the police. She wrote down her name, alongside Leo's and Simon's with the registration of the car. Then she included Arcas' name and number for good measure.

"I don't hear you."

She jumped.

"I'm nervous weeing with an audience."

"Hurry the fuck up or I'm coming in there!"

Savannah shuddered, forcing herself to relax her muscles. Eventually, she weed into the bowl, nearly weeping with relief. Winding the paper back up, she folded it neatly into her hand. She thought about leaving it in the cubicle but hesitated. Would someone take it seriously? There was the usual graffiti listing phone numbers 'for good times,' so she was afraid it would be mistaken for a prank.

Maybe she could leave the waitress a tip? Or ask

Leo if she could buy a bottle of water before they left?

Savannah flushed and stepped out, gripping the wads of toilet paper. She looked over as a woman a bit older than her stepped in. They exchanged eye contact.

"My wife is a little sick." Simon put on a charming smile, as if to explain his presence in the ladies' restroom.

Savannah bit her lip. "There's no toilet paper in either stall," she said as the woman approached. "Here, I grabbed the last few squares." She held out the bunched-up toilet paper to the woman, her hand neatly covering the lipstick writing.

"Thanks." The woman frowned, taking it from her before disappearing into the first stall. Savannah didn't dare linger, allowing Simon to lead her back out moments later.

She hoped that the woman would understand.

"I ordered for you," Leo said, looking at them both from the booth he'd found. Savannah attempted to sit facing the restroom entrance, but Leo dragged her down beside him. She schooled her features, trying desperately not to react.

Minutes trickled by.

Savannah took the glass of water offered. Nervously, she looked around as she raised it to her lips to see if the woman had somehow reacted to the message.

Nothing.

"Sit still, woman."

With bated breath, Savannah waited.

When dinner was served, she took her time, pretending to listen to the conversation between Simon and Leo but watching everyone who passed their table with a mixture of fear and dread. What would she do if someone approached them? What would she say?

Half an hour passed. Still, she waited. The food sat like a lead weight in her stomach. She forced herself to eat the burrito even though she wanted to vomit.

Savannah tried to catch the eye of the other people who walked by, but nobody was paying her attention. The meal was coming to an end.

Still, nothing had happened.

Where was the woman? Had she seen the message?

She watched Leo drink his beer, hoping to prolong the meal, but he was obviously itching to keep moving. She couldn't stall forever.

Fear gripped her limbs now, making her movements jerky and stiff. Nobody was coming to save her. Nobody knew where she was. Nobody—

Savannah jumped as a baby's piercing wail silenced the diners momentarily.

"That's a definite sign to get moving." Leo drained his beer. "Ready?" he barked, shoving her out of the booth.

She nodded, glancing around, still not seeing the woman from the restroom.

"Low on gas," Simon muttered. "Just going to fill up before we head off."

Leo held her close as they crossed the asphalt to the petrol station beside the diner. They were well into country Victoria. That meant long open patches of land, with only the occasional car on the road, and very few houses in between.

It was completely dark now. Her chances were running out.

Savannah stood between Simon and Leo as he filled up petrol, mind whirring.

"How much longer until we get there?"

"'Bout sixty minutes."

Too long.

Now. She had to do it now.

Savannah glanced across the strip of road. None of the cars parked nearby were moving; no one was leaving at the same time they were. But there, in the distance, she spotted headlights.

When Simon headed inside to pay, she knew she had to take her chance.

Now.

Go.

Run.

Savannah tripped, wrenching her arm out of Leo's as he leaned forward to open the car door. She leapt up off the ground, yanking off her heels. Terror seized her arms and legs, throwing off her balance. She would crawl her way home if she had to.

"What the fuck?" she heard Leo roar.

It wasn't long before she heard Simon behind her.

If she could get to that truck, if she could get someone to stop, then maybe she could convince them. The air burned in her lungs, and her legs pumped furiously. Her feet were being ripped by the asphalt beneath her, but she didn't care.

All Savannah knew was that if she were caught, she'd be a dead woman. She ran, the approaching headlights driving her on. But she wasn't fast and she could sense Leo and Simon closing the distance. She sobbed, feeling herself slowing down.

"No!" Savannah screamed, racing towards the main road. She was so close.

All she could hear was the heavy breathing behind her, the rushing feet.

She gulped in air, fighting the nausea, fighting the fatigue. The loud blast of the gun nearly brought her to her knees.

Help me. Help me.

Somebody help me.

Arcas, I love you.

Help me.

Savannah jumped the low silver barrier and fled to the far side of the road.

In the distance, she saw the truck coming. She crossed the median strip and ran straight towards the large vehicle, its lights her saving grace.

Please help me.

The truck didn't slow down. Neither did she.

Please he—

Chapter Fifteen

I t took a few more sightings before Arcas was able to converse with the dragon.

Once she realized that he proved no threat, it seemed that Vanna was curious. It began with her studying him from the air.

Next came her watchful gaze from the mountaintop.

And when she dared to approach him, it was when he had woken from a deep slumber to see her sitting close, staring at him.

From then, they entered into a routine. At sunrise and sunset, she would visit him, and before long, he was comfortable enough to tell her his thoughts. Vanna listened in silence, but her eyes were bright with understanding.

It was in the early morning light of the second week that she approached, opening her wings for him to climb on her back. Willingly, he scrambled up onto a rock face, reaching out to her glistening black scales.

"Are you sure you wish this?"

Her nod of encouragement was all he needed. Arcas clambered on her back, grabbing her wing joint to seat himself eagerly at the base of her neck.

Ready for adventure.

When Vanna soared up to the sky, Arcas released an almighty shout.

He had not experienced such freedom in an age. The thrilling force of her power shocked him, turning his arousal into a consuming tidal wave. The rushing speed stole his breath.

She was magnificent.

It wasn't just the soft scales and sinewy muscle. It was the pulsing power around her, the faint blue glow that encompassed them as they flew through the air that captivated him. He had fought the bloodiest of battles, scaled the sheerest of cliff faces, but found the adrenaline coursing through him—and the slight tremor of fear that accompanied riding upon Vanna's mighty back—profoundly new.

They swirled through the darkening skies. When she tipped them upside down, he shouted, surprised and thrilled in equal measure, glad for his strong grip holding him in place.

Arcas reached his free hand out, skimming the water below, disturbing the shoal of fish darting beneath the surface, then flicked it onto Vanna's neck. She righted them both, shaking off the droplets.

You are a brave warrior.

He nearly toppled off her back and into the inky

river below. Her voice was smooth and low, silky like the velvet oceans that surrounded the mountains afar.

You did not think dragons could speak?

Arcas felt the vibrations between his legs. He had heard the rumors; they all had. There were whispers among the elders, talk of the men and women who could converse with the fierce protectors of sky and sea. Those able to communicate with dragons.

"I have heard of such tales but to experience it is yet another matter entirely."

We speak many different tongues, but we are selective to whom we speak.

Understanding bloomed in Arcas' mind. Of course it wasn't the skill of humans, some magic bestowed on them at birth or wisdom acquired through decades of study, but the power of the dragons. They were the ones who chose.

It made the dragons an even more impressive species. Arcas was drawn to her, to what she could offer. What he could learn.

"But why me?"

He sensed the ripple beneath him, a subtle shiver across her warm scales.

Only the pure of heart, the most valiant and true, receive the dragon's word. It is a reward. A gift. An offer never to be rescinded.

She was in his head. The communication was not spoken aloud, but in a voice in his head.

"Do you speak with your tongue?"

When I've a need to. But linking minds is far easier. Especially when we are up so high.

They could have been in the outer reaches of the planet. His body and mind were anchored to this wondrous being who was able to speak to him. No, who had chosen to speak to him.

More than the honors of battle and war, this was by far the greatest gift he had received. For it was given without him fighting or raging, without him proving his mettle and worth. It was given to *him*. Arcas of Three Waters.

By grace, and not by his deeds, had she chosen him.

He wondered if this was not some elaborate dream.

You are under no spell. This is no dream.

"You read minds as well?"

I anticipate human thought. That, dear Arcas, is greater than any mind reading known to man or god.

He shivered.

And yes, I know your name. I know a great many things.

Of that he was certain.

And so, they flew up along the hills, skimming the pregnant clouds, grey and fat with promise. When the steady patter of rain turned heavy, Vanna landed on a narrow ledge, perched at the opening of a large cave.

She led him through to what he discovered was a series of caves, an interconnected sequence of archways and gates. A small stream laced through one, trickling with water, soothing and soft against the jagged edges of the rock. Another was rough and dry, making tricky to traverse because of the rising stalagmites from the cave floor. He made a mental note that he must return to it, to sit awhile and admire its beauty. The rushing waterfall cascading over the fine yellow grain of the limestone had a magical quality to it.

But Vanna walked with purpose to the center. She drew in a gentle breath and brought the cave to light, kindling a burning fire with her breath, warming Arcas' skin.

Vanna tossed the fish she had caught on the fire, the one she had plucked from the river, easy as you please, as they had skimmed the water. To help, Arcas broke off a tall and narrow stalactite, using it to turn the fish as it cooked.

Before long, they were feasting, man and dragon, together.

He shook his head. Feasting in a cave with a dragon who could communicate with him . . . It was shocking and other-worldly, but exciting nonetheless.

It was then that it struck him. Why he had come.

Not for the promise of gold or riches, but to save a dragon.

This purpose, it was greater than himself and all else he had endured.

Rest awhile. I will keep us safe.

Minutes passed. So he did.

"So how long do you live for?" Arcas stood beside her in the shallow water, waiting for the fish to return. They had spent the day talking, flying, exploring.

He was adept at hunting, had learned how to do so out of necessity, but hunting with Vanna was in itself a lesson. Whether it be lycans, cows, or coyotes, she maintained patience and moved with speed and stealth, neither of which he had seen before.

Her black scales vibrated slightly, her powers attuned to the slightest movement of earth and sea.

Thousands of years. I am more than a millennium old and just in the midst of adulthood, by your standards.

"That's more lifetimes than I will ever see. What do you do to pass the time?"

We do what many creatures do in a life cycle: hunt, protect our homes, educate ourselves, and find a mate.

Arcas studied her, the sleek black scales, the shining aura around her. The melodic voice was soothing, stirring. "And do you have one?"

A mate? She paused. *No. I am . . .* Vanna turned her head away, and the gesture was filled with such sorrow, its sadness transcended all barriers between them. Arcas fought against the urge to reach out, to soothe.

She struck with such speed, he jumped, off guard, then clapped when two large fish wriggled in her talon.

They were traversing the stream later when he asked. "So, if you have no mate and no eggs to guard, what do you do?"

Vanna looked at him, amusement shining in her eyes. *I read.*

"What? Dragons read?"

Vanna huffed. A puff of smoke emanated from her nostrils. *You were not so shocked at learning a dragon could talk, but somehow one that reads surprises you?*

"I apologize. I meant no disrespect."

You know not the way of the dragon, and for that I cannot feel disappointed nor hurt by your comment. Many come here without an openness to understand. But I see in you, Arcas of Three Waters, something so very different.

As always after hunting, Arcas began threading the fish on the sticks for the fire. "I am interested. I want to know everything, if you will permit me to stay."

In my cave? Her surprise shone through.

"I can return to the mouth of Devil's Keep if it's of discomfort to you. But I do wish to learn your ways. I think perhaps I have a bigger purpose here."

Vanna shook out her wings. The gesture reminded him of a flag rising high and proud in the wind. It was of comfort to him, even if it signaled her mild displeasure.

You do not discomfort me. It is—I am not accustomed to human guests.

"For that, I am sorry."

Do not be. It is not in everyone's nature to open their mind. You are a warrior. But your heart—Vanna reached out, a talon pressing against the amulet around his neck. *It is filled with kindness.*

Arcas was torn between embarrassment and denial. "Many in this lifetime would not have said Arcas of Three Waters was kind."

You have seen much bloodshed, you have fought in great battles, but your heart is caring. That is a mark of kindness, even if you do not see it.

Arcas rubbed at the amulet. He had once thought he had rid himself of all softness. At one time he had. When he saw his parents burn, the village up in flames, he had not been strong or capable enough to save them. He had spent his life proving his worth, atoning for his loss. But the years had shown him a different way, a new path.

Yes, he had fought, had spent years travelling with mighty armies, battling one evil then another. But he was weary of fighting. He wished for more.

"It isn't many who see it, Vanna."

She shifted closer now. He was surprised when her wing folded around him. He was taken by her warmth, the glowing comfort of it, yes, but beneath that was an elemental awareness of her, of her aura, that shining blue glow that seemed to seep into his soul in gradual degrees with every passing day.

He could smell her. It was as if all the elements had formed together and existed as one: the ash and smoke of a summer fire, the dewy grass of a verdant spring, the richly turned earth of autumn, and the cool winter wind. It existed all as one in her. How one creature could be all, encompass all in her scent, he knew not, but it called to him. She did so in a way that was beyond ego, beyond the need to prove herself in any way.

Arcas was soothed by the smell. Beneath it, there was a honey-sweet aroma that fed more than just his appetite.

When Vanna shifted back, he fisted his hands on his legs. Restraint. He could not give in to this desire to draw her close.

She was a dragon. A stranger.

And he merely a man.

Chapter Sixteen

Savannah was fifteen again.

She had rushed through her chores, made sure that her siblings were happily occupied before stealing out to the field closest to home where she could read her book without being caught. Without feeling guilty.

Or dirty.

Or sinful.

She stole a glance over her shoulder before settling beneath the red stringybark. She had nearly been caught once before by the boy from church. Leo hadn't questioned her about her book, and given that her parents hadn't demanded she turn it over, her secret had been safe with him.

Her lips twisted at the funny look he had given her in biology class. Leo seemed to always be watching out for her, always there. It was odd, being noticed that way. Looked at not for her sins, but just because.

Mindful of the time, Savannah opened her satchel and shifted the worn bible— because she could never be too careful— taking out the second-hand copy of Love and Honor.

A small pang of remorse left her squirming uncomfortably. It was the first actually sinful thing she had ever done. Stealing the book had been wrong. She knew that. But there was something about it that drew her in. Something about it that fed into every one of her 'wicked' fantasies. One day, she promised herself, she would make it right.

But thoughts of a bright future seemed so far away. If she ever wanted freedom, she would have to run away. And while she wanted to just hitch a ride out of town with the next tourist that

drove by, she knew she had to be smart
about it. To bide her time.

Savannah's stomach rumbled, but she
had learned to ignore the pain. Her parents were making her fast again.

She needed to be rid of her sins, they
had told her. She rather thought a burger
might be a better idea. She had tasted one
once, at the fish and chip shop in town
where the normal kids hung out. It had
been mouth-wateringly delicious.

Even now, her mouth salivated at the
thought.

In the mood for drama, Savannah
found the chapter she wanted, the part
when Maddern broke Emmaline's heart.

"You know I have nearly finished my studies.
Once I leave Oxford, I will be bound for London." Maddern glanced at Emmaline's soft face,
the golden-brown curls kissing the nape of her neck.

The years only seemed to heighten her beauty.

"I do. I hear that your father is very proud."

"That he is."

Emmaline looked up at him, eyes misting. And for the life of him, he could not say the words. He longed to, he thought to, but his father's demands hammered through him, warning him to obey. Threatening him if he did not.

"I have missed you, William."

"And I you, Emmaline."

Unable to control himself, William reached out, brushing the stray curl from her cheek. And then he was cupping that cheek, drawing closer to her.

His lips hovered above hers. He was lost in the depths of her eyes, taken by the sweet candor of her spirit.

"May I?"

Emmaline nodded. "You will be my first."

And his fingers shook a little at that. He wanted to make it pleasant for them both. He took her mouth gently, savoring the taste, the way she sighed on his lips. He felt a frisson of danger, that this be the cusp of something more.

"Emmaline." They broke apart, chests heaving.

"Perhaps you can call upon me when I am next in London, visiting my aunt?"

"In London?" William echoed.

"Just as we used to, as children."

William stepped back once. Then again.

Confound it! What was he doing? He had meant to break it off gently. To sever their friendship and any possibility of a future together, not kiss her.

"My apologies."

"Apologies?"

"I did not come here to kiss you, but to bid you goodbye. For good."

Emmaline placed her fingers on her lips, eyes filling now with tears.

"What we have shared, our friendship, can be nothing more. You can mean nothing more to me. Indeed"—he gasped, forcing the words—"you do not mean anything to me. Our relationship is one of friendship. You should not believe otherwise."

The strangled sob, the one she seemed to stifle, nearly brought him to his knees. He was being cruel, but it was necessary.

He trusted his father's advice. That Emmaline's affection had been nothing more than an infatuation, one cultivated throughout their childhood. She was younger than he, still innocent, a touch naïve. Not yet out in society, she was not accustomed to the manner in which well-bred gentlemen behaved. His father would know. His father had experience in such matters. His father—

But then why was she crying so?

"You know that I have valued our friendship for many years, but I am an adult now. I must follow my father's wishes . . . Well, I—that is to say, we . . . It is best that we sever ties now. You and I will not meet again. Our lives will be different. Do you understand me? I will never make an offer to you, Emmaline. I cannot."

She shook her head, backing away.

Maddern did not reach out for her as he wished. He ground his jaws together, steeling himself against the pain. He must be hard. He must be unfeeling.

Emmaline lifted her chin. "You need not trouble yourself on that matter, William. I perfectly understand."

Cursing, William watched her flee.

Oh, to be in love!

Savannah hugged the book to her chest, leaning against the dry stringybark. Impervious to the ants and beetles, she sighed. How she longed for a grand romance. To be madly in love with one person. To know that they would be there for her, protecting and loving her no matter what.

Savannah glanced at the sky and wondered if it would ever happen.

She knew how the story ended for William and Emmaline.

But what about her?

Would she get her happily ever after, too?

The weeks passed. With every sunset, Arcas lost interest in life outside the caves and their surrounds. The mountains, lakes, and fields all became a home to him. A comfort.

But the outside world did not forget.

He discovered that washing his clothes in the stream one day, when he heard the snap of a twig—another's presence in the glade, across the creek.

"Show yourself!" he hollered.

Vanna was asleep. She had confided that she was steadily feeling weaker, that at the approach of the full moon, she always lost her strength.

He waded farther into the stream, unsheathing his weapon. He had taken off his pack but did not wish to double back. He gripped his knife now, ruing his semi-naked state. If the faceless person wished to attack, he would be vulnerable. One arrow through the chest and he would say goodbye to his dragon friend.

"I demand you show yourself," Arcas ordered, approaching the other side of the bank.

The rustling resumed and a rangy looking man appeared, his beard knotted upon a haggard, meager face. His clothes were soiled, but his eyes—they shone with a keen desire and hunger that left Arcas gripping at his knife.

"Good sir, I am lost."

Arcas smelled the lie as sure as the man's filthy clothes. He did not move closer. "You will find naught but wilderness here."

"Perhaps you have lodgings hereabouts?"

"As you see, I am exposed to the elements as are you."

The man flashed a greedy smile. "Mayhap we can find something together then? I am seeking the way to the dragon's lair. Vanna the Dark is rumored to live in these parts."

"Then you would be mistaken, good sir, for we are all alone."

The man studied him, holding his gaze. Arcas did not blink, standing his ground.

"You would not mind if I trespassed across these rivers then?"

"This is free land, but I warn you of wolves and such in passing."

The man ran his tongue along his teeth. "Well, perhaps it best I be on my way."

"That would be wise."

"Good day to you . . . You did not give me your name."

"I did not." Arcas folded his arms, blade glinting.

"So be it," the man responded, returning to the shadows.

Arcas waited a beat then tracked him along the riverbank until he disappeared from view.

A strange presentiment coursed through him as he made his way back, causing him to seemingly wander aimlessly along the bank before returning to the entrance of the caves.

He would be ready when the time came.

Chapter Seventeen

They lay on the bank of the stream, enjoying the last rays of the summer sun. It had been a glorious fortnight, but the vitality, the vibrancy of Vanna's powers was clearly waning with every passing day.

She assured him she wasn't sick, but still, he worried.

"Tell me, Vanna."

She looked up at him, shaking out her wings. *I cannot. Not here. Fly with me.*

Arcas climbed onto her back, pressing his nose in brief contact against her warm scales. She shuddered, an acceptance of him riding her.

I cannot talk of it without pain, so let me take you to the sunset, to see beauty even when I feel hurt.

"Have you been visited often? By man?"

I have been hunted by many, men and women. Creatures of all species wishing to steal fortune or powers. It has made me wary of visitors. You are the first I have had the pleasure of knowing.

She lifted them effortlessly. The rush still left him dizzy, that sudden ascension into the sky. A thrill, a joy, he allowed it to fuel him, the part he had closed off for so long.

"You are my first dragon, so in that we are on an even playing field."

I grow weaker by the full moon. The tales you have heard are true in that regard, and that is when I am plagued most. You see, I was cursed as a young dralig by an evil witch who wished to gain my powers. She had hoped that by cursing me to live in human form for seven days each year, she might hope to best me. To use her powers against mine.

"What happened?"

She tried. For many years, she tried to do so but failed. And I did everything in my power to rid myself of the curse.

"Can you speak to her? Have her release the spell?"

She is dead.

Arcas felt the stabbing regret of it pierce through his heart.

"Fuck."

Yes. I mourned for hundreds of years, wishing that it were not so, hoping that I could somehow reverse such a fate.

"But you still become human?"

Every year, for seven days, I am cursed to be hu-

man. *And every year, people think some maiden has been captured by the wicked evil dragon.*

"And do you . . ." Arcas clenched his legs around her tighter as Vanna dipped and dived around the mountainside. "Is it enjoyable? Being human?"

She shuddered. *It is difficult. I lose my strength, my powers. It feels as though I lose myself. So while, over time, I have learned to live in acceptance of it, the human form . . . it pains me.*"

Arcas gritted his teeth. He heard the anguish and wished that he could do something to alleviate her discomfort.

"I'm so sorry, Vanna."

I have had over a thousand years to grow accustomed to it.

"But it brings you no joy."

No. The confession was a hushed whisper inside his head.

"I do not wish you to fear it: this change. Vanna, I swear to you that I will do everything I can to protect you." He thought of the man who had sought his friend's location. He would not let that happen. "I will remain here with you, my friend."

I believe this is true. But there is something I wish to show you. To share. Come.

Vanna landed on a smaller ledge, the entrance to a cave they had not visited before. She took him down a long tunnel, this one smaller than the other caves. How she managed to fit was surely the work of magic, for it was difficult for him to crawl through the space.

He scraped his knees, knocked his head, struggled to breathe.

When Arcas thought that there was no end to the darkness, a brilliant burst of light appeared. A shaft of sunlight, breaking through the rock, shone directly down on the contents on the cave.

Arcas shielded his eyes.

Brilliant, shining gold.

My treasure. She motioned with her wing for him to proceed. Arcas glanced at the gold, nodding, then paused. Walking up to get a closer look, he realized that the gold bars were actually spines. Thousands and thousands of spines. Of books.

And the tickling humor rang from the depths of his belly until he was gasping for breath, his laughter echoing around the cavernous rock.

Vanna's treasure was not jewels, but golden-bound books.

I had no use of jewels and trinkets. But books . . . Arcas realized by her tone that she was embarrassed, perhaps even hurt by his laughter. *Books are worth more to me than pieces of metal.*

"Vanna." He approached, taking her talon in his hand. "I laugh not at you, but in thinking of all those men and women out there lusting after your treasure, risking life and limb for what they see as caves full of bounty, to find books instead of bars. I think it wonderful."

She huffed, joy suffusing her eyes. *So, you think it not odd?*

"It's brilliant." He grinned.

She motioned for him to continue. Arcas perused the spines, marveling that the titles, too, were engraved into the gold.

"This must have taken a long time."

Not once I realized how to do it. After many decades of watching the smithy at his work in the cover of dark, I chanced it. I burned many books in the making. But finally, I did this.

"May I touch them?"

Of course, she breathed.

Arcas picked up a book, one of poems. He found a smooth rock to sit on and opened the page to read:

> "When love gives itself unbound
>   By sight, by form, by time—"

Vanna continued.

> *When love flows true*
> *Across realms and rivers.*
> *Caught not by fae or form.*

Together they finished.

> "When love sees like,
>   Through winters to springs,
>   Therein true gold lies —
> The purest of love, the purest of hearts
>   A promise

Forever entwined."

Their voices reverberated across the rocky walls, hanging in invisible lines of verse in the limestone cavern, as solemn as prayer. As striking as the silvery stars in the night sky.

It is one of my favorites.

"I can see why." Arcas' heart beat a strong, steady pounding, shaking all his foundations. A spark, one that extended from his breast to hers, had been ignited. He could not look away. The expression on her face, the beauty emanating from her, rendered him speechless.

He stroked at the words on the page.

You like it?

"Fucking aye."

Chapter Eighteen

Arcas groaned, the pain at his shoulder rousing him from his unconscious state.

"The wound . . . it is deep." Vanna tended to him, but he could hear her concern even through the calm.

A fire roared in the distance, but it was the searing heat in his bones that left him shivering and shaking.

The slimy bastard had returned. With six other men.

"What happened?" Arcas fought to move but cursed at the heavy weight of his limbs.

I was awoken from a deep slumber. I knew something was wrong. The connection we share was calling me to rise. To find you. When I did, I found you lying by the river beside the other men, blood and weapons strewn along the bank. They were all dead. I-I thought you were dead too.

Arcas blinked, remembering the ambush. One

moment, he had been fishing, and the next, he had been attacked by mercenaries come to find the dragon and her treasure.

There had been too many men to fight, enough to wear out even the most seasoned of warriors, but a fierce protectiveness had stolen his reason. As if he had had the strength of a thousand men and the valiant heart of a dragon, he had fought until he had been bloody and spent.

And if not for Vanna finding him, for her gentle and shrewd care, he knew with utmost certainty he would now be in another place alongside his poor mother and father.

But Arcas knew, he would do it again. To protect her.

He stroked at her nose, warm and soft, his muscles burning from the exertion. Vanna gave him a gentle lick on his palm in answer.

You fought valiantly, Arcas of Three Waters.

"It is what friends do."

He heard her voice. It was what guided him through the night. It soothed him. Stirred him.

When Arcas awoke again, he felt more than comfort. He was consumed by a great need. He ignored the longing in his loins, for what could he do?

She was a dragon. He a man. All between them would be forbidden. Futile.

He did not wish to pain her with yet another human taking what was not his—she had been violated all her life by mankind. He would not add to her suffering.

But as the days passed and his strength returned, Arcas craved movement. When he began to feel restless in the caves, he once more rode out with her, eager to feel the sun on face.

But when his desire stirred, he found it difficult to ignore. Nevertheless, he averted his eyes when she bathed in the cool waters, the droplets running down her smooth black scales, her eyes blue and bonny in pleasure.

She was a dragon. He was a man.

That was all they would ever be.

You showed me a great honor. Vanna spoke, harking back to the battle he had fought, her voice smooth and deep as always inside his head.

"I did what any warrior would do. What any friend would do."

No man I have known across centuries has shown me such respect. For that, I thank you. For making my cave truly a home.

Embarrassed by her sincerity, Arcas looked away. "If we are in the way of showing gratitude, then I thank you for taking me in. For tending to my wounds."

Vanna bowed her neck. *It is nothing. What any friend would do.* She bared her teeth and Arcas was struck by the playful expression, the gleaming happiness from her eyes. *In truth,* she continued, *if the change were not so close, you would have been restored in hours, not days. And I fear perhaps more will come.*

"What change?"

Her smile was shy. *There is something I have not told you. Of what happens when I turn into a woman.*

Arcas winced as the echoes of pain reverberated through his shoulder. He shifted to focus on her eyes. They never failed to draw him in, as did her spirit. "Yes?"

She huffed and he sensed her embarrassment.

"You can tell me all, Vanna. I will not fear it."

Vanna ushered them to the grassy bank beside the river. When they were settled, she began.

When I turn, I become . . . hmm. I begin a period of need. I will be in heat.

"Heat? As in . . ."

I will wish to mate.

Arcas raised his eyebrows, studying her profile.

"Watch me, Vanna. When you speak, look at me."

A few moments passed before she did.

"Tell me of this heat."

It lasts the seven days. I . . . I seek men to lie with during that time from different towns. Or I did at first when I was very young. But the experience has not been so pleasant. Some did not survive the mating.

Arcas gripped her talon in his fist, enjoying the stinging bite of pain in his palm. "Have they taken advantage?"

Many have. And so I bear the heat in my own agony, in my own way.

"Fuck."

It was long ago. Many hundreds of years. And I have grown accustomed to dealing with intruders in my caves, even in my weakened state.

"And what of the heat?" Arcas shifted, ignoring the dull ache in his ribs. Her soothing words, a chanting rhythm, eased his discomfort.

Give it time, brave Arcas of Three Waters. Healing well takes time.

"Distract me then. Tell me of the heat."

What do you wish to know?

"Can you—have you—had offspring?"

He felt the sadness in her. Her scales cooled; her body deflated.

No. If I am to bear draligs, then the curse says I can only conceive in human form. The seed would die if I am a dragon in my natural state, hence the power of the curse. For no man can satisfy the heat, the craving for fulfilment. No man can sire a dralig.

The sorrow inside him for her was powerful. As was the hatred for the bitter witch who had cursed her. To live without the pleasures of the body, to not ever be fulfilled must be a thousand deaths in life.

"What of"—he grunted—"other dragons?"

Vanna shook her head, derision in her tone. *No dragon wishes to mate with the cursed one. They can sense that something is not right with me.*

Arcas shifted closer. "Vanna, I am sorry. I will stay with you. I will protect you."

I know, dear friend. And that to me is more comfort than I have had these many years.

Chapter Nineteen

S avannah started, a cold sweat gripping her chest.

"Shh, it's okay. I'm here." Arcas sat beside her, his hand in hers.

For a second, she thought she was still fifteen, stuck in the nightmare that was her childhood, powerless and unable to change her fate. Seeking solace in the only thing that had ever brought her joy. The only thing that brought her joy *then*. But everything had changed since. She was no longer stuck in Bellingham, no longer punished for wanting to do all the normal things teenagers craved.

"What the fuck happened?" she croaked, her mouth dry and odd, as if she had chewed on cotton wool for hours.

"You don't remember?"

"The truck. Leo. Simon." She glanced around them then winced as the pain radiated through her head.

"They're in police custody. You got a nasty knock from throwing yourself at the truck. You landed pretty hard."

"Why do I feel like I've been asleep for years?"

"You have. Well, not years, but they gave you a sedative. You were . . ."

"Hysterical. I remember. I was petrified."

"But you're safe. And I'm here. You did good, Van. You did fucking brilliant leaving those clues. And writing the word help on your hand made the truck driver suspicious of what was going on, enough to get him and his buddy to help you to the police station."

"I can only remember bits of them being in the truck with me. I was so frightened, I think I blacked out. I haven't fainted so much in my life."

"Terror will do that to you."

"I just can't believe I was kidnapped."

"Are you up for chatting about it?"

Savannah nodded, recounting everything that happened.

"I just wanted to come home to you. That's what kept me going."

Arcas brushed at her tears. "I'm sorry I couldn't save you, Van. I could only get the number plates. But they were able to track you, at least, with that. And the woman's call from the diner. That made all the difference too."

"He wanted to marry me."

"What?"

"Leo was taking me somewhere to get hitched. He's fucking deranged." Her voice shook with anger.

"Leo?"

"You know, the guy I told you about."

"Which one?"

"We grew up together in Bellingham. He was my first kiss. We attended the same church. He seemed really protective. After all the shit that happened, I thought it meant that he cared. But he got it in his head that we were meant to be. He was the one who was sending those pictures."

"The one who followed us at Fantasy Core?"

Savannah glanced at him as all the pieces slid into place. "Yes."

It wasn't her brother. It had been Leo all along. "I never want to go back there again."

"To Bellingham?"

"Yes. I never want to see that place ever again." She gasped, body trembling.

"You're safe," Arcas soothed, kissing her finger-tips. "You won't. Ever. I've got you, Van. You're safe. I'm here."

"Mum?"

When Savannah awoke later, two figures stood beside her bed. For a second, she had thought she was a young girl, awoken by a strange, scary dream, searching for comfort. Even in the dark, she recognized their silhouettes.

"Dad?"

She sat up, rubbing her face. She was no longer a child. No longer an innocent. Savannah shuddered as the events of the past twenty-four hours rolled through her. With bleary eyes, she picked up the remote on her bed, increasing the overhead light.

Blinking, she stared at her parents in shock. They were here. Actually here. At the hospital.

She froze when her mother's face crumpled. "We heard what happened."

A raw swell of emotion seized her throat, making it impossible to speak. Savannah reached instead for the water by her bed and took a sip.

"Who told you?" she squeaked.

"Your brother," her dad offered.

Maybe she had got it all wrong. Maybe they really did care. After all these years, after all this time, maybe they had come to realize how much they loved their daughter. How wrong they had been.

Here they were now, at the hospital, showing her support. Something she hadn't received from them in . . . ever.

"We couldn't believe what happened."

"Me either. It was terrifying."

"But why?" Her mother pleaded.

Savannah frowned. Why *wouldn't* she find being kidnapped terrifying?

"We just don't understand it," her father said,

Vixen

shaking his head. Savannah looked at him, the grey
creeping in at the temples, the frown lines forming
deeper creases than had been there before. A strong
feeling of sentiment threatened to overwhelm her.

"We wanted to come and see you. To
understand."

Savannah glanced between them. There was
something in her mother's voice, the look in her father's eye, that left an eerie buzzing sensation along
her forearms. That heavy, familiar feeling of dread
was sickeningly present. Again.

"Understand what? He's deranged." Savannah
picked at a stray thread of the hospital blanket. Her
heart thumped once, slow and heavy.

"He could have been so good for you." Her
mother shook her head.

And just like that, the vice around her lungs
crushed her feeble attempts at reason. Her pulse was
scrambling now, fear distorting the rose-gold image
she had painted only moments before.

But that was all that it was. An image. A lie.

One she so desperately wanted to believe. That
hurt more than anything else. Because she thought
she had grown past this.

"We want to know why you didn't accept his offer
of marriage, Savannah. Leo loves you. He'll take care
of you, give you babies, bring you back home just like
a good Christian would do. He'll help save your soul."

Savannah gaped at her mother, staring back at the
woman who thought that accepting the hand of a

stranger who had kidnapped her was some sort of holy gesture.

Her father leaned forward. "He asked my permission, and I gave it freely. You should reconsider. Tell them you were mistaken and get that boy out from that holding cell. You can make this right, Savannah. You can have a life that Jesus wants for you. A life with your family."

Her mother reached out. Savannah jerked her arm away.

"Just to clarify, you want me to go to the police, tell them to release Leo, the man who stalked and kidnapped me, the man who tried to force me to marry him against my will, because it's the—"

"What the fuck?"

Savannah trembled, looking up at Arcas as he wheeled into the room, his eyes serious.

"What the fuck is going on here?" Arcas sat beside her, reaching out to grip her hand. "Are you okay, Van?"

She nodded but held on. "My parents thought it would be best if I just forgot the part where Leo kidnapped me. Oh, and once I get over that trauma, they think I should drop all charges, and—wait for it—accept his hand in holy matrimony."

"We would have convinced her if you hadn't shown up."

"You don't get it," Savannah interrupted before either of them could continue. "I have no interest in Leo. I certainly don't *love* Leo. The man is deranged. I don't want anything to do with him, now or in the future."

"If you can't respect that, you should just leave." Arcas' voice was now steely.

"Like hell we're leaving!" her dad bellowed. "You need to send that freak away and come back home with us. We can save you from your sin, from your whoring, girl."

"Watch how you speak to your daughter or you'll be flat on your ass, sir."

"This!" Her father pointed his finger, his face turning red. "This is the degenerate you want to live with? You could have a good man, Savannah. A good, *Christian* man, one who follows Jesus' path. And instead, you choose *this?*"

"Look at what you're doing to this family!" Her mother's shrill reply hit a nerve.

Savannah snapped. "What I'm doing? What the fuck is wrong with you? Do you even hear what you're saying? Never mind this bullshit request for me to marry my kidnapper, what about all the other shit ways you've destroyed this family? Hmm? How about pretending like your daughter wasn't abused as a child? How about punishing me for displaying normal child behavior? How about the million ways you were never there for me?

"I thought you actually gave a damn. And that's the sad, sorry truth of it."

"What's going on here?" A nurse rushed in,

drawn by the raised voices. She was followed closely by what looked like hospital security.

Her mother turned to her. Savannah could have sworn she saw remorse flit across her face. But after a moment, it was gone, and with it, Savannah knew, any sliver of hope that their relationship could be repaired.

Her mother's eyes gleamed with intensity now. "We do care, child. For your soul. You'll be living in eternal damnation. The devil comes to kill, steal, and destroy. And baby, that half-man you're living with —*in sin*—is the very devil. But you can be saved. Leo can save you. Don't you see?"

"Enough! You need to leave. And please don't come back. Don't contact me. Don't call. I don't want to see you ever again. We're done."

"Excuse me, ma'am, sir. You need to leave," the nurse interjected. "You cannot come here distressing our patients."

"Savan—"

"Leave," Arcas ordered. "Now."

"You need to move along, folks. Or I will take action." The security guard loomed over her parents.

"You're making a big mistake." Her father shook his head.

"Then I know I'm doing the right thing," Savannah replied, chin held high. "I'm doing this for me." Savannah looked at Arcas. "For us."

Chapter Twenty

And then came the change.

And everything Arcas had told himself flew from his mind faster than a soaring eagle.

The days were turning, and while the warmth of summer still lingered in the day, the nights were cool. Autumn was fast approaching.

Vanna had grown weaker and weaker until he was forced to feed her to maintain her strength, to keep her from a deep slumber. He was beyond weary, but it was the persistent fear that pulsed beneath his skin that kept him alert. Arcas witnessed her pain and sat beside her, reading lines of poetry, stroking her sensitive wings until he, too, fell into a restless sleep.

When he woke, it was past evening. Vanna had gone.

"Vanna!" He called for her in the cave. His heart gave a frantic jig, throat clogged with emotion. He stepped out into the inky night, the full moon an ever-watchful eye.

And then he heard the singing.

Arcas knew that voice, even from miles away. He was drawn to it.

The stream.

A stabbing disappointment sliced through his chest when he came upon her.

For before him was not Vanna, his dark-scaled dragon beauty. In her place was Vanna the woman, with hair as dark as her scales trailing down her naked back.

"Vanna," he whispered.

She turned, breasts swaying. She was curved and lush and everything inside of him desired her with a fierce longing that he could not ignore.

He wanted her. As dragon. As woman. As everything he had not dared to give himself. Because beneath the exterior was Vanna. And everything in her drew him in, something he had not believed possible.

She covered herself now, head dipping in the shy manner of hers. She may have been in human form, but all he saw was the dragon.

"No. Do not cover yourself." His voice was thick, his hunger a heavy cloud of need. She must see it. Surely, she must feel it, this yearning he had for her. This unspoken ache in his loins, yes, but deeper than that.

For her.

Arcas approached carefully. Though she seemed brimming with vitality, he could not shake the weakened form of her from his mind. "Are you well, Vanna?"

"Now that the change has taken place, I am. But I am hungry."

"I can hunt. Rest awhile on the bank. There are—"

Her blue eyes, potent and powerful as the aura that surrounded her, flashed. "Not for food."

Arcas' cock leapt. He could not mistake her meaning. He did not imagine that expression. He understood her passion, a mirror to his own.

"Vanna." He breathed. "Are you—"

"I need you, Arcas. As a man. A lover. I will go wild for the wanting."

He stormed through the water, consumed by the searing desire to taste her.

She turned to him, back straight, head raised, the Dragon Queen that she was, meeting him with the same fierce desire.

And oh, the glory. The pleasure of it shimmered through him. He shuddered as his mouth fused to hers. He cupped her face, using his mouth, teeth, tongue to kiss her. He could not reel in this passion. It poured out in this connection to her.

"Touch me," he groaned, pulling her against him. "Take your fill. I am yours, Vanna the Valiant."

When her nails, sharp and pointed, raked down

his back, he cried out. The pleasure-pain seared through him. Even as the scratches wept, he craved more. He wanted her fierce and fiery, unbound by fear.

He needed to see her in all her glory every day, for all time. To sate her desire until they were spent and then do it all over again.

Vanna cupped him, and he almost saw stars. Her round breasts, the dark tips pebbled against his chest, the yielding mouth, soft and sweet . . . She drove him mad. He would gladly fall into that abyss for her.

Arcas strained against her hand but shifted back, restraining himself.

Carrying her now, he placed her on the grassy bank, shedding his trousers. Vanna was glorious in the moonlight, his dark dragon of a woman.

He sucked at her breasts, palming the heavy weight, feasting at the smooth, soft skin. What would her scales feel like when aroused?

"You're beautiful."

He trailed kisses down her stomach, to the curling dark hair between her thighs. The honey-sweet scent enticed him, and the first lick had her hips arching.

"Oh!" Her thighs trembled. "What . . . What is this?" she panted.

"This is the pleasure I give to you."

Arcas' cock wept with every sigh, every moan. He lapped at her, loving the way her hips rolled.

"I did not . . . It's never been . . ."

"Not like this?"

She shook her head, eyes pooling with tears.

"Yes, Arcas, more."

So he gave and gave, taking her to the precipice and rearing back, building a maddening desire for her. The muscles in her legs began to quiver, her moans vibrated through him, and with it the satisfaction she was straining for grew stronger.

Vanna began to thrash and gyrate, her sharp nails digging into his fragile skin, her words unintelligible and pleading.

Only then did he take her over the edge, letting her fly. She broke over his mouth, shuddering and shaking, breasts bouncing as she came on his tongue. And what poured from her was the same blue aura, a bright liquid that coated the ground between them.

It made him harder than iron.

He wanted to feel that warmth soaking his cock, to pump into her and have her gush and squirm in pleasure.

"More," she panted. "Here." She pressed his hand lower, to her entrance, still wet.

"Fuck."

He didn't need to be asked twice. Gripping her hips, Arcas positioned himself.

"Wait."

He bit back an oath, grinding his teeth with restraint. "Tell me."

"When it is the mating . . . you, your—"

Ida Brady

"Cock," he supplied through gritted teeth.

"It locks into my . . . You cannot unlock. It is the mating heat, the curse that distracts me from all else except desire."

"I want it. I want you, in all forms, with any curse. I want you, Vanna."

"Then take me," she sobbed, crying out in pleasure as he did.

The first thrust had him seeing stars.

She may have been in female form, but the circled ridges inside of her, the tight bands that gripped his cock, were not human. He rocked over her, marveling at the new sensation. Every inch of him was squeezed, every part consumed by this pleasure.

Gladly, he leaned towards her, gripping her hands, pinning them into the wet grass as he fucked her.

When her legs wrapped around his waist, he felt as a king would taking his queen. Her breasts skimmed his torso, soft and seductive. Her cries filled his ears, taking his desire to heights unseen.

And when Vanna's gentle mewling turned to ragged, indiscernible cries, he knew he was close.

"I cannot hold off."

"Nor I." She shuddered then jerked, flooding his cock with wet warmth.

"Vanna!" he cried out, gasping when his cock locked into her, deeper now. He could not thrust, for he was kept in place, but she was somehow milking him, drawing his cock in and out inside of her.

Arcas shuddered at the pressure, the pleasurable release. In it was an intensity he knew he would never experience again. And the aura, the soft blue glow, emanated around her, her liquid coating his cock.

In Vanna, he was lost.

Chapter Twenty-One

S avannah gave her statement to the police, making sure they knew what had happened, recounting every step of the way.

It was a difficult process, but it was made so much easier by Arcas' presence. He never left her side. He was her rock, staying with her until the doctors cleared her to return home the following week.

He was patient and kind, holding her when she woke in a cold sweat, taking time off work just to be close to her, cancelling the next Fantasy Core session until she was ready to get back into it all.

As the weeks passed and life began to find some sense of normalcy, Savannah was beginning to understand herself and her relationship with Arcas in a way she never did before.

"What?" She looked up from her place on the sofa, closing *Love and Honor* just at the final, heart-wrenching scene. She hadn't wanted to rush re-

reading it. She was learning that some things were better left sampled slowly instead of devouring it.

Huh. She was learning to be patient after all.

"Nothing." Arcas smiled but continued to stare at her.

Savannah felt the rush, that wonderous warmth that flooded her heart now. He was looking at her like *that*. And while his expression wasn't lustful, dear lord it made her want to climb on his lap and devour him whole.

There was a new tenderness between them. A softness in their relationship that came from going through shit together and coming out stronger on the other side.

"Spill." Savannah scooted closer, running her hands through Arcas' dark hair, delighting in the way he looked. The way he looked at her.

"This year has been epic. And before you ask, in a hot *and* not so shit-hot way."

She squeezed the hand he offered as the painful memories snatched her serenity.

"It has."

"And I know this is going to sound batshit crazy, but I think it's made what we have so much stronger. It's made me come to terms with things in my own life that I thought I had resolved. But now I know I truly have made peace with where I'm at. Who I am. And it's because of you, Van.

"You've shown me what it means to be vulnerable and open. The thought of losing you really fucked me over. I was so afraid that I wouldn't get to see your smile, to watch you fall asleep, hell, to explore some wild new kink . . . but beneath all that was me realizing how much I love you. And need you. I never, ever want to live my life without you, Savannah.

"And if that means I get the chance to show you how I feel about you, that I get to even spend another minute in your life, then I'll consider myself the luckiest fucking man in the whole world."

Savannah's eyes filled. "Five hundred twenty-five thousand six hundred minutes. Times a million."

For all her obsession with the Duke, for all her fantasies of nineteenth-century heroes and old-fashioned courtship, not one line of *Love and Honor* could have compared to the sentiment Arcas had expressed. To her.

And Savannah knew that no matter what happened, beyond any fantasy, beyond any work of fiction, that the reality of their love meant that they would be able to work through it all.

Together.

Chapter Twenty-Two

Arcas' heart was heavy.

With every passing hour, Vanna grew weak again, the change back to her natural form draining her energy, diminishing her spirit.

Though they had fucked for seven days and nights, swapping stories and sharing food, though their passion had consumed him with every drawing breath, Arcas would give it all up to spare her the pain she was in now.

He never knew this powerful desire to protect another, not on this level. Vanna's pain was his. Her heart beat as if it were his own.

They had made the cave their home. Arcas had ventured into the village once for necessities but did not wish to leave her, the memories of the invaders still fresh in his mind.

As the nights turned and the wind grew bitter, Arcas found himself imagining a life with Vanna, flying and riding. Without war or greed. A simple life of pleasure and discovery.

And every night, he dreamed of her—fucking her, watching the pleasure on her face, doing what seemed natural and right.

He woke as he did most mornings, with his cock standing to attention, straining against his clothes, seeking sweet oblivion. Seeking her.

Eyes still closed, Arcas freed himself, sighing as his fingers closed around the base of his cock. He took his time, imagining burying himself inside her. A trickle of awareness made his hand pause mid-stroke. Arcas opened his eyes and looked across at Vanna.

Her eyes were open, watching him. Her nostrils flared. She was back in her natural form.

I can smell you. If you are willing, I wish to lie with you.

"Vanna, you have been in my dreams. Not as a woman, but as you are now, a dragon. I want you, if we can—" He gestured between them.

Vanna huffed, her voice serious. *We can. I think. But from what I have heard, there is immense pain. For you.*

"Tell me." He sat up, watching her, wanting her, his cock tall between them.

Mating between species is frowned upon.

"But not uncommon?"

Vanna bowed her head. *No. Not uncommon. But not without pain.*

"I have dealt with pain my whole life, Vanna. For you, for this, I would risk it."

It is said that you will split inside of me.

Arcas' eyebrows rose. "My . . ." He gestured.

Yes. You see, I have two entrances.

Arcas rubbed at his face again, processing it all. "Two?"

She huffed once more, a chuckle this time. *In human form, you would not have noticed. But in my natural state, well, I require two cocks. Which means you must*—she paused—*split in two.*

"Sounds painful." But even knowing it, even accepting that there would be pain, he felt a yearning, a need far greater to join with her. Man to dragon. Arcas to Vanna. He accepted all that she was in her natural form. He wished to know, to join with her now that she was recovered from the change. He would willingly take any pain for the chance at loving her. "I'm in."

This time she did laugh, a sweet rolling sound from her belly. Something inside of him shifted.

I am serious. This will not be easy. Folklore suggests a man and dragon can mate, but that you will be engorged and split. There will be two cocks that will lock inside me. As before.

"Show me," he murmured, approaching her. He stroked her scales, the soft, dark ridges warm under his touch. "You are beautiful, Vanna." He looked up at her, blue eyes wary but warm. "I want to experience everything with you."

Even dual penetration?

"You can do that?"

My tail inside your . . .

"And this gives you pleasure?"

Immensely.

"Yes." Arcas stripped off his clothes. He picked up where he left off, palming himself in slow, sure strokes. "As you can see, I am ready for it."

He closed the distance between them. The honey-sweet scent clawed at his need, driving him to touch her, hold her. Arcas kissed her scales, swirling his tongue along the smooth edges, licking in turn at the six dark nipples on her underside, enjoying the huff of breath as she exhaled. He continued sucking and biting until her tail swished and she shuddered in impatience.

His fingers followed suit, rubbing at her nipples until she sighed.

She held a power in her limbs that vibrated at his touch. But in this, in being with him like this, he saw her strength, the vulnerability behind that power. And he craved more.

Vanna swished her tail and lifted it up and out. Arcas stood behind her, stroking it, enjoying the way it curled and shimmered. Her aura was even more powerful; it danced around her, beckoning him.

Touch me. She shifted, exposing herself to him.

Arcas marveled at the wetness that surrounded her dark skin. The entrance to her sex was hidden under the base of her tail, as soft as her silky underbelly.

Vanna shuddered at his first, tentative stroke of her sex. He circled her now, enjoying the way she sighed.

He lifted his fingers to his nostrils, breathing her scent, and was overcome. Lust, the strong, hot force of it, punched through him. She smelled as sweet as the wildflowers that grew on the mountaintop, earthy as the ground beneath their feet. A heady aroma lured him in. He licked one wet, sticky finger and found her flavor as good as any brew he had supped.

And now he would have her.

Naked, vulnerable and out of his mind with longing, Arcas stood. Gripping her tail, he angled his rampant cock toward her, entering her slowly, achingly slowly.

He felt the resistance against his tip, as though he were being crushed by the weight of her. She was painfully tight and for a second, as hot as lava. Nevertheless, Arcas thrust inside of her, shaking from pleasure.

It wasn't so—

Arcas roared. The transformation began.

Arcas. I am so sorry. He heard Vanna's sorrowful voice in his mind, and he gnashed his teeth together, gripping her tail from the pain.

His cock thickened, lengthened, and split. He could barely breathe from the searing pain that rendered him in two. What seemed like hours passed in mere minutes.

When his cock stopped growing, he shuddered, heavy and burning. The throbbing continued until he seemed to latch on to something pillowy and soft deep inside her. It surrounded him from base to tips, for he had two cocks now. He could sense each of them, cocooned inside of her warmth, independent and yet connected. The soft ridges inside her gripped him, and the pleasure shot up his spine, all the way back down to his toes. Arcas had never experienced such a wonder as this.

Blessedly, the pain ebbed away until there was nothing left but the sweet sound of Vanna's satisfaction as he nestled balls deep inside of her.

He was heavier, thicker, and longer than he thought possible.

Oh. Vanna's sigh of satisfaction sliced the curse off his tongue before it had the chance to flee his mouth. *It worked. You are my chosen. My mate, Arcas of Three Waters.*

The rhyme. How had he forgotten the old crone's prophecy?

> If love be sworn,
> If love be true,
> The curse once bound
> Shall break in two.

Arcas gasped, overcome by pleasure, unable to

speak. It coursed up through him, and even as she pumped his cocks, his natural instinct was to thrust. He did so, rutting her now in the most basic, primal way.

He was a dragon. He felt it in his mind, in his limbs, this coupling between them transforming him. He wished it so.

Are you well, Arcas?

I am. Vanna, I am your mate. I am yours, the chosen.

And so, they fucked.

Vanna lay down on her back, with Arcas straddling her above, touching and tasting until they were both sweaty and drenched.

The pressure and sensation were beyond his imagination. He existed as a man, but as a dragon too, with his mind connected to her, able to speak to her just as she did him. They were mated. Bonded. Connected as one.

Are you ready, Arcas?

Arcas watched in fascination as her tail transformed, the spear-ended tip rounded out, curved, soft and glistening with the same blue wetness as she had before.

Yes. I want to experience everything.

Arcas didn't know if he could take more pleasure. He was longing to come inside her, wanting to fill her with his seed, to see the pleasure mark her face as she came.

He sucked at the tail she offered. It was thick and

wet and tasted of the same honey-sweetness that he had come to learn was her own unique essence.

He felt the intrusion, the pressing nudge at his rear.

Vanna's eyes held his, watchful. *Are you certain?*

Arcas' voice was strong, sure. *I am.*

And then she was seeking entry, a twirling, drilling arrow stretching his ass, easing inside him until he thought he would black out from the sensation. He was full. So very full he could not seem to draw breath.

But Arcas stood on shaking legs, and while his cock pounded into her, he was pounded too. She fucked his ass in a relentless rhythm, working in tandem so that he was simultaneously filling and being filled. And when the tip of her tail nudged the sensitive area inside him, he nearly did black out. The power of it, the unrelenting pleasure and pressure were so strong, he was incapable of coherent thought.

Arcas panted, sweat dripping from his torso, his eyes locked on the beautiful blue gaze of the dragon beneath him.

He existed for this sensation, chased the jolts of pleasure until he did not think he could stand it any longer.

Arcas cursed and muttered, the build up in his balls a fire blazing out of him. It consumed not just his cocks, but his whole body. The pleasure radiated from him, skimming along every inch of his overheated skin. When he came, his passion echoed around the cave, the intensity of his seed spilling inside her beyond his comprehension.

Before he could blink, Vanna shuddered. With a mighty roar that shook the walls of the cave, she, too, came, scales shiny and slick. She erupted inside of him, expelling a ball of fire from her mouth at the same moment she drenched his cocks, a powerful reminder of what she was, what he had experienced.

And the aura that shone around her surrounded him now as well. It was surprisingly cool. But then he felt it, akin to a key turning in a lock: the connection between them shifted into place. They were joined both body and spirit. And the same light that came from her, came from him too.

They were one. Whole.

And together, as one, they slept.

Sexcapades – Vanna the Valiant

Never in a million years would I have thought I'd be a dragon.

Never in a billion years would I have thought I'd be a dragon that falls in love.

But. Let. Me. Tell. You.

Sex as a dragon, getting double dicked by the warrior hero as you fuck his ass, is next level.

Total boss move.

Hardcore porn got nothing on monster love.

Which, hello, has opened up a new kink in my life.

One which has made my boyfriend and me a lot more vulnerable than I had ever thought possible. Sharing in the secret, wonderous thing that turns my boyfriend on has made me appreciate how much trust we have built. And in that, how the very desires of our heart can play out in a nonjudgmental way, in a nonjudgmental fantasy world.

Because of it, I think I can understand the emotion behind the kink, which makes sex with my boyfriend crazy hot. Because aren't kinks just secret needs we otherwise feel too embarrassed to reveal? But when we do . . . holy hell, it's the most fulfilling thing you could do. It unlocks a new awareness of your desires, both physically and emotionally.

And you know, I'm always up for a new kink.

Is dragon edgeplay even a thing? Only one way to find out, I suppose . . .

A wicked 9/10 on the O-meter.

Yours,

The Gamer's Girlfriend

Chapter Twenty-Three

*S*he would never see his face again.

Emmaline closed her eyes against the pain.
To block the memory from her view. But all she
could see was him, standing tall and stiff at the steps of
Everton Hall as she bid him goodbye. The tightening of
his jaw. The burning intensity of his gaze. That final
touch, that covetous look . . .

Emmaline opened her eyes and cursed. She was
back in Wiltshire and miles away from the Duke. Her
duke.

She would need to become accustomed to this. It
was for the best. She knew it was for the best. But she
longed for him. She ached for him. It had been three
days of hollow pain, three days of mourning. She tried
her best to conceal her feelings, but her aunt's knowing
looks proved that she would have to try harder.

Try as she might, Emmaline could not replace the
feeling of loss when she thought of William. Even
though they had parted as she had requested, it did not

assuage the stabbing longing that stole her breath every time she thought of him.

Which was always.

She supposed there was some satisfaction knowing that Lady Dewberry had been wrong. There had been no grand announcement. The final ball of the house party had been uneventful. And bittersweet.

William had insisted she stand beside him in the receiving line, welcoming each of the guests who had attended. It appeared he had invited most of his neighbors and many of his tenants to the ball, and he took the pain to introduce her to each and every one of them. Emmaline had been impressed at how he had taken his responsibilities so seriously. And how each guest in turn had admired and respected him.

Had she not known any better, she would have thought he had been courting her. William had been as he once was: open and attentive. He had sought her out at every opportunity, affording her a glimpse of the boy she once knew.

But still, she knew it could not work. And so, she had remained steadfast. It was a world she would never occupy. Not by birth or marriage.

Now, Emmaline wandered across the field beside the church, picking up a stray stick, dragging it behind her as she was wont to do as a child. But as she looked out across the quiet landscape, the open green fields did nothing to capture her heart. She may be home, but she felt a stranger in these parts.

With heartache, she swatted at the low-lying grass.

Even her plans to visit her sister, to distract herself with new amusements, had been dashed just this morning with their unexpected arrival.

They had announced they planned to stay for one whole week. And with her aunt and uncle in residence for yet a few more days before they themselves returned home, the house was positively bursting with people. Merriment and chatter were in every room, when all Emmaline craved was a moment of peace.

Sighing, she crossed the field, making her way back home. Prayer had been futile and unhelpful, as her soul was already damned by the Duke. But her body . . . oh! How her body burned for his touch. She had prayed the Lord's Prayer perhaps a little more excessively on Sunday, as though that could save her from her sins.

Emmaline passed the small school on the hill, newly opened. The vicar had boasted of its success, too, on Sunday. She had humored him for a good while, remembering his attentions to her long ago, but was not moved. While he was affable and kind, her heart was now with William.

As it would always be.

Crossing over the stone bridge that signaled the way home, she glanced down at the gentle-flowing river. She shivered at her feeble attempts to find peace. She must not give up. She must be more determined.

What she needed was a plan. She could not change her past, but she was her own woman and, fallen or not, she must rally again.

She would simply have to live alongside the pain in her heart.

Perhaps she could convince her sister and Lord Fanworth to take a week in Bath? That would be diverting. She had never been to Bath. She could take the waters and promenade in the Assembly Rooms.

Feeling a sliver of hope, Emmaline glanced up, spotting a carriage in front of her home. She sighed. Yet another visitor. Shielding her eyes from the afternoon sun, she took her time walking back, occupied by thoughts of the new diversion. There was the Royal Crescent and the Pulteney Bridge. Mayhap she could—

Oh! She recognized that carriage. Indeed, wicked sinner that she was, she knew the detail of its upholstery shockingly well.

She gripped the low-lying gate that separated her from her childhood home, mind racing. She fumbled with the latch, cursing as she opened it. Then, she was through and racing across the lawn, into the house.

Voices. In the drawing room.

Emmaline flew through the door, only to stop short.

She recognized those broad shoulders. Though they were clothed in a many-caped travelling coat, and though his back was turned, she knew him instinctively.

He turned.

And she was blinded. Not by the low-setting sun piercing through the open window, nor by his dazzling good looks, but by the love that blurred her vision. The force of it would have toppled her backwards had she not been clinging to the back of the settee.

Merciful heavens, what was William doing here?

"Emmaline."

She blinked through the confusion, approaching him now as if she were in a dream.

"Your Grace."

She glanced beyond Maddern, to where her father had risen. He stood stiffly to the side. The Duke, too, was serious.

"Tea?" *she proffered, hoping to dispel whatever lurked in the air.*

"Sit down, daughter. I wish to speak to you."

Wary, Emmaline took a moment then sat beside her father on the settee, William on the one opposite. Three days seemed a lifetime. Now that he sat before her, proud and devastatingly handsome, the sorrow she felt was even more acute.

"As you see, the Duke has kindly paid us a visit. I believe that—"

"Oh, child, there you are! We were almost about to send word for you." *Her aunt, the Duchess of Carrington, sailed into the drawing room. Then she stopped short, eyes rounding in what appeared to be surprise.* "Your Grace, so very good to see you! You have come to pay us a special visit?" *She sat on the far end of the settee, beside William, seemingly oblivious to her father's scowl.* "Will you be staying for tea?"

"I—"

"You know, I was just this moment telling my"

sister of your splendid house party. Everton Hall is just divine."

"I am very pleased you enjoyed your stay."

"Indeed, as were many of your tenants. You know, Mr. Collins, His Grace gave us a tour of his estate one day. He was most attentive to Emmaline, explaining to her all that occupied his time as the Duke of Maddern. It was remarkable to see how seriously he took his responsibilities."

Maddern demurred, "I thank you, duchess. It was but a trifle."

"But indeed. It was evident what a fine job you have done since your father's passing. Such a testament to your good character."

Emmaline glanced at William, noting the way his eyes warmed. Her aunt's favor was not lost on them. Her father's scowl seemed to indicate it was not lost on him, too.

"That is very well for his tenants," her father responded. "However, the Duke, Emmaline, and I wish to discuss a private matter, Lady Carrington. If you would kindly—"

"Excuse the interruption. I say, Maddern? Is that you?" Lord Fanworth entered now, eager and amiable. "I thought I recognized your carriage outside."

"Yes, indeed."

"It is very good to see you again."

"And I you."

"You know, Mr. Collins," Fanworth continued, sitting in between her aunt and the Duke, "I have been *very fortunate to call Maddern my friend. There I was, ready to marry Anne, and with no one to stand up with me. Do you know, had it not been for Maddern's help at the last minute, our wedding would have been a disaster. Honorable, was it not, to come to our aid?"*

William coughed. Emmaline was certain it was to hide an ill-timed laugh.

She did not know whether to be mortified or highly amused. Hovering between both, she stood. "I shall ring for tea."

Beside her, her father bristled.

The others ignored him.

"Oh, yes, do," agreed her aunt, barely glancing at her brother-in-law.

Emmaline arranged the tea table in readiness.

"Back to the issue at hand," interrupted Mr. Collins, breaking up their conversation. "His Grace has kindly paid us a visit. He wishes to speak to Emmaline on the matter of marriage."

"Marriage, my dear?" her mother interrupted, bearing the tea tray herself.

Emmaline sat mystified. William wished to speak to her of marriage with her entire family in attendance?

Her father looked exasperated. He did not even nod to Anne or her uncle when they, too, sailed in. "And I suppose you three are come to sing the Duke's praises?" He glowered at three guilty looking faces.

"Well, Emmaline has been telling me such wonderful things about the improvements on Everton Hall *since I last visited, Papa. In addition to His Grace's generosity."*

"And it was most generous of him to take all the gentlemen hunting during our time there. Do you know, he keeps a very-well stocked home wood?"

"I have heard plenty on his generosity, rest assured. However, there is still the matter of marriage that I wish to discuss."

Her mother's eyes rounded. "Oh! Are we to congratulate you, daughter?"

Her father interceded. "I have not given my—"

"Husband! How could you refuse such a man?" her mother chided.

"I have—"

"Indeed, he really is a capital fellow," her uncle proffered.

"You do not—"

"Oh, Papa, Emmaline deserves—"

"Enough!" Her father stood, face flushed. "I implore you—all of you—to please desist. I have yet to speak upon this matter." He raised his hand to silence any eager intrusions. "What I wished to say, what I had hoped to say to the Duke and to Emmaline before we were interrupted by this very poor theatrical display, is this: I have withdrawn my objections to the match.

"Indeed, on the matter, I must tell you—all of you —that I have come to realize I have made an error in my judgement." Her father turned and sat beside her. After a moment, he took her hands in his. His lined

face showed no signs of anger. Instead, he was calm, at peace. "I realized, with the help of others"—he glanced at her aunt—"that I upset you in London, child, and for that, I am sorry. I still see you as the sixteen-year-old girl in need of protection, and I forget that you are now a woman, free to give your heart to any gentleman you please.

"I have been blinded by my own experience, my own prejudice, but to continue to cling to my fears would be remiss. Doing so would be in contrast to securing your happiness, which is all a father should ever want for his children. Your dear mother once gave up her title and her fortune to marry me. I saw how cruel society could be and I did not wish that for you. But time has altered many things, but in it, my love for you remains constant. I was blinded by my prejudice. And for that, I am sorry."

Emmaline's eyes filled. She held onto her father's hands, heartened by his confession, at the sudden turn of events. She had his blessing. His love and support. Relief flooded through her.

"Perhaps I was too quick to dismiss the Duke's affections for you," her father continued. "But after our discussion today, and the many notes of correspondence on the matter that I have received from His Grace, in addition to the many letters certain individuals in this room have sent," he remarked, eyebrows raised, "I am left in no doubt of his feelings."

Marriage? Feelings? What feelings? Emmaline glanced at the Duke. William had never declared any-

thing but a deep, all-consuming passion for her. Yes, he cared for her well-being, of that she was certain, but she had been fooled into believing his feelings meant something more once before. She was wiser now. Wary still.

"I thank you, Papa, for your words, but as I am yet to know of such feelings, I cannot make a decision."

Her father cleared his throat. "That is for the Duke to tell you. In private."

William stood, bowing. "I thank you for your blessing, Mr. Collins. Indeed, I thank you all for your support. But I believe it is time I speak with Emmaline alone."

He extended his hand. Emmaline took it, walking out of the drawing room on unsteady legs.

Six beaming smiles followed her. And one fatherly look of pride.

Emmaline shivered, her mind whirling at the sudden turn of events. One moment, she had been planning her trip to Bath, and the next, she was in imminent expectation of a proposal. From spinster to duchess, she could scarce draw breath.

"What is the meaning of this, Your Grace?" she questioned as they reached the privacy of the gardens outside. "We agreed under the ash tree that our dalliance would end, just as the house party would. I am confused at the sudden change."

"I thought it best that I speak to your father first. In person. Letters can sometimes fail at conveying one's true feelings. But your father has proven obstinate in my plans."

She blinked, absorbing this new information. "Your plans . . ."

William drew her close. "My dear, sweet Emmaline. The past three days have been agony. Watching you leave Everton was a pain I could not bear. But I could not speak then. I had arrangements to make. I could not declare myself without knowing your family would consent. That I could claim you as my duchess."

"Not Lady Dewberry?"

The Duke huffed in disdain. "No, not Lady Dewberry. Never her. I made certain she knew of my intentions towards you. Her grand plans were never truly set on me in the first place."

"I am not so certain of that, but I am glad to hear it."

"You must know my relationship with her ended long ago. I have never, nor ever will feel for her what I feel for you."

"Tell me."

She wanted to hear it all.

"You were right. What you said under the ash tree that day, everything. I have behaved as a cad, and I wanted to make amends. You have always been my duchess. Nobody, no other soul in the world would fit the title, no one other than you."

She? Always his duchess?

"Walcott," she breathed. He had been trying to tell her all along.

William's mouth twisted. "Walcott was never one for keeping secrets, but he does what he thinks is best."

"I had thought . . . Oh, this is too much." She could not bear the exquisite anticipation. It raced along her body now, lighting up her senses.

"Emmaline, I wanted to declare my feelings then," he continued, "but I knew I had to secure your father's approval. Your uncle was helping me in this matter, but it took some time. I did not want you to have to choose between love for your family and your life as my duchess. I know you well enough to know it would be a bittersweet marriage if they did not support you. And so, I needed to seek your father's approval, to do this right, before making you mine."

Joy burst through her now at his tender words. Joy and disbelief that William was here, declaring himself to her, saying the words she had longed for all this time.

"And as per this afternoon's display, your aunt thought it imperative that they all pitch in, lest your father remain objectionable." He laughed now.

"I thought they had taken leave of their senses."

"They wished to show their love for you. And in doing so, they afford me a great honor."

She saw the pride in his eyes, felt the warmth in his touch. It thwarted every doubt that lurked in the shadows.

"Emmaline, I have loved you as a boy, and now as a man. I cannot live another day without knowing you are mine." He cupped her face, brushing at the tears that fell.

"I do not want you as my mistress, but as my wife. Say you will accept, dear Emmaline. Say you will be my duchess?"

"William . . ." Her throat closed over. She took a moment to bathe in the love she could see in his eyes, to revel in the words he spoke. She could almost burst from the happiness pulsing through her. "I love you. These past three days, weeks, months, have taught me that nowhere is home to me without you by my side."

She drew breath to utter what was in her heart, to give what she had desired for so long. "I will be your duchess, William. I am yours. And you are mine."

She tilted her face, gripping his coat as his mouth covered hers, his kiss warming her, thrilling her, promising to her a future she had never thought possible.

For Emmaline was no longer lost, no longer caught between two worlds. Now, she had found herself, her home, with the one man who had captured her heart. The one man who vowed to cherish it.

And for the first time in a decade, Emmaline felt whole.

For the first time, she found peace.

For in his arms, she was loved.

Chapter Twenty-Four

Sexcapades – A Happy Ending or A New Beginning?

ow do you measure a year?

In Sexcapades? In books read? In new kinks or declarations of love? Or do you spend your time so caught up in all of the above that you don't even stop to pause and reflect?

If you have been following this blog, you would know that I love nothing more than a good romp in the sack.

But today, I'm in a reflective mood. And while this year-long sex challenge started off as a physical exploration, I must confess, the past few months have been eye-opening.

The demons from my past have forced me to face things I'd rather forget, but in doing so, I've learned something so fucking valuable. And listen up 'coz it's the motherfucking key to all this magic. It's the one thing that will never change.

And that's the love that I have for myself. To make hard decisions. To explore my body on my terms. I'm able to understand what I need and desire in a way I didn't before. On a deeper level than I ever thought possible. Because I've accepted myself—every flaw, every fear—and have come out the other side knowing I'm worth every bit of that love.

But what's more—and perhaps the biggest thing of all —is that I've discovered that in loving all the parts of me, I'm so much more free than I was before.

Free to fuck any way I choose. Free to discover new kinks. Free to fall even harder in love with my boyfriend.

Because, as I've discovered, you can't really love someone fully if you don't love yourself first.

What I'm saying is that when love enters the equation, oftentimes the sex is off the charts amazing. I'm ashamed to admit that all my previous relationships lacked the deep trust that I share with my boyfriend. While our relationship is open, it's also based on commitment and love.

So while I've enjoyed being plundered by random men and women at Orgy House, while I've been titillated by my online sex with strangers or screwing myself senseless as Emmaline with the Duke, I have to say, my strengthening relationship with my boyfriend has given me even greater pleasure.

How is that possible? How is it that fucking strangers and discovering new kinks has brought us closer together?

It feeds our love. It feeds my soul. And I've never been happier.

Sex and love and the wonderful world of fantasies . . . I challenge you, dear reader, to take the plunge, to give it a red-hot romping go. Take the opportunity to tap into the core part of you, that hidden need or unexplored fantasy. Bask in all that self-love.

You never know what wonderful parts of yourself you just might discover.

Another 10/10 on the O-meter.

Yours,

The Gamer's Girlfriend

Want to grab exclusive content, bonus scenes and giveaways?
Click here to sign up to my newsletter, With You in Romance.

Also By Ida Brady

The Gamer's Girlfriend Series

Book 1

Virtue

Book 2

Voyeur

Book 3

Vixen

Teacher Chronicles Series

Before You Were Mine

When You Were Mine

If You Were Mine (Coming 2023)

A Sweet, Sexy, Scandalous Series

Sweet Spot

Sex and the Stage

Secrets and Scandals

Standalones

To Tango with Love

The Gamer's Girlfriend Series
Book 1

Virtue (Amazon)
Virtue (All Other Retailers)
Book 2
Voyeur (Amazon)
Voyeur (All Other Retailers)
Book 3
Vixen (Amazon)
Vixen (All Other Retailers)

About the Author

Ida Brady writes contemporary romance novels that promise humour, heartbreak and a happily ever after. With all the sexy bits! A lover of chocolate (milk or dark) and thunderstorms (the bigger the better), she's usually dreaming about her next cast of characters or what she's going to eat for her next meal. When she isn't trying to tame her intractable curls, she's running after her kids, usually with a book in hand.

Ida lives in Melbourne with her Irish husband and their out-of-control collection of books. She sometimes daydreams about having a huge library in her apartment but will settle for stacking novels in the kitchen drawers instead. In her past life, she taught VCE Literature and English to a gaggle of teenagers. While she misses their enthusiasm, she sure as hell doesn't miss marking papers. You might find her dancing the sexy Argentine tango in her spare time, which isn't very often these days. She loves travelling with her family, observing strangers at café's, and getting lost in a good story.

Want to hear more?

Visit: http://www.idabrady.com or sign up to my

Newsletter, With You in Romance for giveaways and prizes!
Follow me on Tiktok, Facebook! and Instagram or leave a review on Goodreads.

SUBSCRIBE FOR ALL THE NEWS!

If you want exclusive access to giveaways, sales, and new release alerts first, then subscribe to my monthly newsletter, With You in Romance at www.idabrady.com

Acknowledgments

It's DONE! Book 3 is out at last and I'm filled with a mix of relief and sadness. I've loved working on this series and have adored getting to know all my characters. I'm so lucky to be able to write what I love and in doing so, sharing these stories with you. For all those who have taken a chance on this series, or left a review, thank you!! I still pinch myself when I think about all the readers who have shown an interest in my books. Every new book is another exciting adventure.

To Team Brida: Brian, Adria, Niamh and Hugo. I can say I'm the luckiest woman in the world to have you all in my corner. All that love and support, not to mention sweet little hugs, have kept this sleep-deprived mamma going when some days it was just bloody tough. Love you all to the moon and back! Here is to our next big overseas adventure!

To Hilary, my Alpha reader, editor and friend: THANK YOU! Your encouragement, dedication and support throughout the many iterations of this series has been phenomenal. It's time for cocktails and Thai food, girl.

To Norma Gambini: you remain a treasure to work

with. You have been so very encouraging throughout the years and I'm so grateful you stuck with me and believed in me. Thank you so much for your editing prowess. I'm so lucky that I get to work with you. Like I always say, you're the best!

To Tash: a million thank yous for all the wonderful work on my covers. I cannot gush over them enough. You have a gift!!

To Ebony: formatter guru and all-around awesome person. Thanks SO much for all your work over the years. You're a gem to work with and an absolute life-saver on those deadlines.

To my extended family: thank you for always believing in me. I write this with a twinge of sadness, surrounded by moving boxes as we start our new overseas adventure, but know that I am always grateful for all you do, for all of your unwavering love and support over the years.

To my wonderful writer friends, my Meetup girls: your advice, feedback and general support really makes me feel like I can do this. I wouldn't be where I am without your friendship and support, so thank you! Here's to another release, and hopefully another retreat down the track, perhaps the next one across the wild Atlantic.

To my BETA readers: your time, effort and insight make me feel super lucky to have you all in my life. Thank you for all the feedback, encouragement, and support. Y'all ROCK!

Finally, to my readers: whoever you are, wherever you may be, I hope that this novel gives you a chance to escape from reality, even if for a chapter or two.

With you in romance,

Ida Brady